PARADISE LOST

&

THE WATCHERS OF HEAVEN

TCHINDA FABRICE MBUNA

BOOK ONE

THE GREAT REBELLION

REVELATION 12:7-17

Published by Tchinda Mbuna Books
Published in United States
2023

Copyright © 2023 by Tchinda Fabrice Mbuna

www.tmbunabooks.com

DEDICATION

To Her Excellency of my heart,
In my heart's weed, she weeds.
In my heart's weed, she is the wit
Of what my heart delights with.

To Her Excellency of my heart,
Blessed is the day we did meet.
I can assure you; she isn't a mitt.
In all storms, she can cope or fit.

In all my heart's squares, she fits
The mother queen of love in her outfit.
Always classic, not to be a misfit,
And always on heels, never bare feet.

She's Bessi, but call her Madam Mbuna.
She's all in one, pretty like a Mbuna.
You can also call her the real Miss Angel,
Everything about her is of a divine angel.

When you give her love,
She multiplies and gives you more.
When you give her peace,
She does increase your peace and grease!

She's my heart's garden flower.
Which gladdens my heart forever!
More peace and love that will never
Be drained by chagrin or by any means severed.

Bessi, your love is treasured,
Noble and even lettered.
You made our love a nest, so secretive
Like Blue Jays, you are daring and protective.

You fight with the might of a crowned eagle
Who else deserves such honor or regal?
What is of your equal – raven, cockatoo, or crow?
You're the finest of all, and will always glow!

Also, to them all; my sons and daughters,
Wendy, Katriel, Samuel, Karen, my laughter.
You've made me a happy father.
My heart is delighted to see you grow farther.

I have begun a trip; you must keep the journey,
Life is a journey, not always sweet as honey.
Never a bed of roses will it ever be
As prophesied, though contracted with a rose.

You will see racism, injustice; don't bother.
Keep moving, keep loving each other.
Be each other's keeper as an honored potter,
Bear each other's burdens and avoid unnecessary
pother.'

You are the arrows of my youthful vitality,
Be the light of the world; avoid whimsicality.
Be the salt of the Earth, the pride of morality,
Be the glory of the world, the pride of divinity.

Do good all the time; life is full of eventuality,
For God has endowed in you grace of hospitality.
When you age, age with graceful vitality,
But never forget life hereafter or immortality.

Your father, Mbuna!
Your best friend, Mbuna!
Endless love from
Tchinda Fabrice Mbuna!

ACKNOWLEDGMENT

My acknowledgment is a debt of gratitude.
Gratitude to all for their positive attitude.
Writing this book was more journey
A journey is not always very sweet as honey.

I am only a branch from a tree with many parts.
A tree has many branches as an entire part.
And not a sole branch, entirely apart.
Writing this work required more than an art.

To my parents
Mr. John Mbuna and Ms. Helen Mbuza

Your voice remains an interior force of motivation.
Your love remains an interior force of conviction.
You sowed the seed of this art from childhood.
Which has remained today even In my adulthood.

My gratitude today is for your beatitude.
My gratitude today is for your positive attitude.
My gratitude today is for making me who I am.
I am grateful to you, and to the I AM WHO I AM.

I say a warm thank you to my artistic mentor,
Awah Oliver Nde, a playwright, poet, and editor.
He is a man of many hats, a literary orator
Screen Writer, Film Maker, and Film Director.

To my professor, Enongene Sone
Professor of English and African Studies.
The Voice of African Mythology and Studies.
The bright and morning star of a new dawn
Thanks for your encouragement down the lawn.

Your encouragement is like watering a flowering lawn
With words of wisdom, and the sagacity of a sage.
You have exalted African Folklore and given it a name.
A name that will remain the African pride and fame.

Dr. Vivian Nkongmenec
Gender/Post Colonial feminist beacon of light.
Thank you for being that light always bright.
The voice of African literary and feminist dignity.
I hail your wit, excellency, reliability, and majesty.

Nkwetatang Sampson Nguekie
Literary mentor and versatile facilitator.
The writer of the art of all ages, a liberator.
An advocate of true art, art in its classicism.
I salute your ingenuity, poet of romanticism.

Rev. Ajebe Francis, Rev Agbor Cyril Enow
Rev. Walters Akor and many others I know.
I appreciate your love and spiritual aid.
I appreciate your love and spiritual aides.

To Friends, family, and well-wishers
Thank you for always being divine watchers.
I might have enough words of gratitude,
But I have a word to thank you for your attitude.

DRAMATIS PERSONAE

Major Characters

ADAM: First Human Ancestors

EVE: First Woman Ancestor

CHRIST: Second Adam and Messiah.

KING ELOHIM: Creator of The Universe.

LUCIFER: Fallen Royal Guard of Creation.

MICHAEL: Royal Guard of Creation.

GABRIEL: Royal Guard of Creation.

SERAPHIEL: Leader of The Seraphim.

REBEL: Group of Rebellious Angelic Hosts.

WATCHERS: Group of Arch Angels or Higher Ranks.

ELDERS: Empyrean Heaven Worship Leaders.

METATRON: Voice-over Narrator (Elohim's Scribe).

Minor Characters

MERKABAH: Chariot of Elohim

BEELZEBUB: Second Commander in Chief of Lucifer.

BELIAL: Lucifer's First Lieutenant.

GOTHMOG: Lucifer's First Front-Line Lieutenant,

Leader of all the Balfrogs.

FOREWORD

God releases men who will keep the literary flames burning with his will for the nations and all planets in every generation. But when some generations get skipped because those, he gave wisdom slept, he raises in other generations, cross-generational writers, to whom he gives wisdom and carries them through circles of life by revelation, so they might echo his hidden or ignored will and truth. Mbuna Fabrice Tchinda is one of such young men, whom God put in his pen missile bullets which tear through every generation with divine revelations.

Paradise Lost and the Watchers of Heaven Book One is a play that cuts across the generations of mankind before, during, and after creation. The Hidden revelations which even Biblical Scholars and Clerics are either adamant to believe or say, are released in a powerful revelational style.

From the Prologue to the Epilogue, he travels with the Holy Spirit from when God begins his creation of the Heavens and Celestial beings. He captures the war for Elohim's throne by presenting full flesh battles that can only be seen in the likes of *Avatar, Spartacus, Troy Scotland,* and *Rome* as he presents a large army of fallen Angels led by Arch Angel Lucifer and God's Army led by Arch Angel Michael in which Christ is the Captain of the Hosts.

This introduces the genesis of every modern Science which man only discovered… as projected in Ecclesiastes 1:9

"That which has been is what will be,
That which is done is what will be done,
And there is nothing new under the sun."

He captures the patience and forgiving nature of Elohim the creator, for his recalcitrant and rebellious children through his history of creation, then his intentions, and the creation of the Earth. Then the making of the hero of mankind – Adam, through which he paints the genesis of all jealousies, controversies, conspiracies, and battles surrounding human life from birth till maturity.

A reading of the book **Paradise Lost and the Watchers of Heaven Book One** will keep every human being spellbound. As you get to read your own story and find where you are in life and where you are going. Deep revelations about Elohim and his creations are brought to the lamb light in highly poetic dialogues and stage directions.

It is a book of self-discovery for every generation of humans to read and find their places in creation. After reading through, the clergy will develop a stronger understanding of God. It is a book to read again, a play to watch again, and a movie to watch again and be born again. Amen…

The Editor
Awah Oliver Nde.
(Playwright, Poet, Editor,
Screen Writer and Film Maker).

In my proud opinion, the beautiful ones have already been born. Consequently, the best way to make yourself more beautiful than them is to ardently appreciate their beauty with words or actions. Nowadays, Science and Technology claim to be advancing more than ever before, yet, wisdom, especially divine wisdom, is steadily declining. Modern man is fast becoming a dunce. He only knows that one can only reap greatness from doing something new. He is ignorant that one can equally reap greatness from reminding people of an old thing in an artistic manner. That's why art is invincible.

Such was The Renaissance, which caught the attention of the whole world and became the leading artistic movement for the larger part of the fourteenth century to the seventeenth century. Michelangelo's painting of The Creation of Adam, and Leonardo da Vinci's painting of The Last Supper of Jesus Christ and his twelve disciples, was a typical example of reaping greatness by reminding people of old things in an artistic manner.

This is exactly the kind of greatness which Tchinda Fabrice Mbuna has reaped from reminding us about the story of God's creation of the universe and Lucifer's attempted insurgence and final submergence. This book, **Paradise Lost & the Watchers of Heaven**, is the prelude to a more radical renaissance than the former. How many of us are ready for this renaissance?

In one of my publications on romanticism titled *The Prologue to my Lifetime Creative Writing Career in the Writers' Retreat countryside*, I underscore the absolute necessity for universality in the writing of a classic. By my reckoning, no African literary work has the pedigree of a classic because all African writers are afraid of handling universal subjects in their works.

They remain, local heroes, because they find comfort in handling local subjects, especially the conflict between antiquity and modernism, African culture and western culture, the living, and the dead. This notwithstanding, here comes an African-American writer, Tchinda Fabrice Mbuna who has distinguished himself from the madding crowd, and mustered the courage to take up the challenge against universality.

How many African writers would mention God and heaven in their literary works? All they would fashion would be to call an illiterate enchanter "Wise One." If he is that wise, why can't he use his wisdom in looking for himself a lucrative job and living in a cozy mansion rather than living in the bush, putting on haggard clothing and battling with mosquitoes and climatic hazards? By and large, Mbuna's contention is that we must remind ourselves of the need to evolve in our respective walks of life.

We are not evolving. Writers are not evolving. They are stagnant. Moribundity is eating to their fabric like a cankerworm. He is not only using words to lead this radical renaissance for the *summum bonum* of all and sundry. He is also using action. All his books are demonstrating that long-awaited departure from the yoke of traditional conventions. And we must read them day and night in order to be passengers aboard this Zion Train.

Nkwetatang Sampson Nguekie,
Literary Mentor and Versatile Facilitator,
Bamenda, Cameroon, March 2023.

PRELUDE TO THE PROLOGUE

I am Tchinda Fabrice Mbuna, a man of clay,
But in Christ, I find immortality's ray.
In this mortal realm, I witness disorder,
The collapse of social order, growing ever bolder.

I may not have seen Eden's fall from grace,
But evil's lustful world, I have to face.
A world where trust is broken and lost,
Mistrust and chaos at an unimaginable cost.

Yet, there is one who witnessed it all,
Metatron, the Archangel standing tall.
He beheld the creation and its inception,
Elohim's presence, the divine connection.

With fiery pillar and immense size,
He saw the war in heaven with his eyes.
A rebellion that he did not endorse,
A pure desire within him to enforce.

With 36 pairs of wings, eyes untold,
He sees all, as heaven's stories unfold.
His face shining brighter than the sun,
A powerful being, though second to none.

Thousands of eyes, like great celestial lights,
Adorning his being, their eternal sights.
A crown of precious stones upon his head,
49 jewels, each like the sun's golden thread.

Lower than Elohim, yet close to His side,
Witnessing the universe, its wonders wide.
Metatron, the divine Archangel so dear,
Experiencing Elohim's love and patience clear.

He comprehends the Three of Eternal Life,
Before paradise was lost, amidst the strife.
He holds the mystery of knowledge's might,
Of good and bad, he shines wisdom's light.

As a divine spokesman and playwright, I stand,
Ready to script a play with Metatron's hand.
So, hold firm, for the ride will be profound,
In "Paradise Lost and the Watchers of Heaven" we'll be
bound.

GENERAL PROLOGUE

[Narrated By Elohim's Scribe]
[The Angel of His Presence]
[The Revealer of Secret and Mysteries]

[Archangel Metatron]

"In The Beginning Of All Beginnings"

I, Metatron, the only living scribe.
I was a witness to what I will describe.
I was chosen to write for future tribes.
All the mysteries I say, to Elohim I ascribe.

Before time even began or its inception
Elohim chose me to witness these revelations.
He instructed me to write his marvelous acts
Which Tchinda F. Mbuna will write in arts or acts.

As one of the angels of his presence
I witnessed the might of his omnipresence.
I wrote down all his acts, ventures at creation
Even the fierce angelic war of emancipation.

I'm Elohim's scribe and keeper of his record.
He is the El-Shaddai, Adonai, he is the Lord.
His deeds and Will were all written in the Torah.
A Tree of Life for humanity and their aura.

Let me tell you the tale of creation and rebellion
When Lucifer rallied with him a great battalion.
Most of them fought with the strength of a lion,
But will be defeated from both heaven and Zion.

Once upon a time, out of space and time,

Was a dazzling light from a height so bright,
To map out a new horizon and space of time.
It was a light that shone from a great height.

No creature could gaze at this throne's direct sight -
None for ages ever got an insight into this light.
On this gigantic throne was lying a book -
The book itself was like a gargantuan logbook.

On it was engraved writings with a flaming pen
The last book, words of this book ended with Amen!
It was called the TORAH, the book of divine life
A book whose texts were sharper than a paper knife.

This throne was pulled by four mighty creatures.
Like humans were their natures and features.
Each had four faces and four warring wings.
With special grace to control even the winds.

Their movements were very strong and swift,
Radiating a bright throne light as the offspring,
of an ancient King, on an invincible throne.
Forces of darkness before them got overthrown.

The legs of these four creatures were all straight.
Days and nights before this throne they did wait.
Their feet beseem those of a calf, strong as bronze.
Four wings had each, beneath these wings human hands.

Each creature had many faces and wings at a glance,
Faces and wings that beseemed beautiful but fierce.
One had the face of a strange human being,
With a motion movement that seems all-seeing.

One's face beseemed that of a roaring lion,
Whose fierceness had been provoked - this lion.

Two others had the face of an ox and an eagle;
Boosting a regeneration of power and might –

Ascending and descending on wheels fire.
Their appearance looked like burning coals or fire
Pulling the throne of light where it required;
Their movement was so bright that it spilled fire.

In every back-and-forth movement was lightning
This dazzling throne and light were of a King,
Whose beginning and end are imaginary unknown.
His voice from the light was soft like that of a drone

And steady was his voice, but not his nature seen.
From nothing, he created the being before his throne,
A potent angelic being was created— Michael
With a shield and sword in the armor of a knight.

Standing by the throne was Lucifer and Gabriel
With the DNA of the invisible King called El...
Two others were created Raphael and Uriel
But amongst these royal guards was darkness.

In the heart of Lucifer was pride, a mortal sin.
He was created perfectly with twelve wings
He was made of fire, the glory of kings.
He envied Adam, with a heart of darkness.

Adam was of clay but was Elohim's righteousness
Lucifer was deposed before Elohim's throne
By Michael, in a single ferocious heavenly combat.
Lucifer was cast down to hell, but he made his throne,

On Earth to overthrow all the sons of the light.
He brought darkness into the world for his delight.
In a vow to destroy Elohim and the sons of light,

For Christ was to shine in Adamic men's lives in light.

He created the New World Order of all ages –
To govern and control kingdoms for ages;
A prince of darkness over God's universe.
A challenger of Adam to live a life in reverse.

He presented to the fallible fallen human race
The New World Order in a way so perverse -
A worldwide conspiracy against Elohim's Grace,
To set every grace for the race of men to reverse.

He ruled the world for years like a lion
Yet was not the lion of Judah or Zion.
This Leopard of darkness, like an eagle, had wings
Cloned with heavenly power but for rebellious spirits.

And his beauty shrunk into the looks of a beast –
Full of anger to have been robbed of heavenly glory
He then really became a ferocious and angry beast;
Who could change like sweet music at a feast.

He had another form of a beast, like a bear
For woe unto mankind, his load imposed to bear.
In his sturdy bear mouth were three ribs
Of victims whom he ate and enjoyed their hips.

Sooner in a flash of light was he a Leopard
With four wings beseeming those of a bird.
He had four heads with the power to rule
For never was he to ever enter the heavens realm.

His teeth were of iron, His limbs and strength powerful
He fakes sometimes, looks great and wonderful.
But his ultimate goal and zeal was ultimate cruelty,
For one cruel in the heavens will worse on Earth in liberty.

His cruelty was subtle, as though with no flaw -
He came to kill, steal, and destroy with pride.
In him was no truth; within evil did reside.
He was the father of lies, and many deceived died.

There came a man with a new name, Jesus Christ -
He brought a new government, but had to pay a prize.
Paradise Lost was to be restored through him -
A slain lamb, the exact image of Elohim.

He came to this world made cruel as the divine light,
In him was the word, the world created by him -
Everything in this wild world was created through him.
He came to his own, who rejected and scorned him.

In the wilderness was a voice testifying of this light.
A voice that wasn't himself, the long-awaited light,
But the voice of redemption, pleading with other's plight;
For He in the lives of men was the original Light.

His sword for human salvation was double and sharp
That slew evil men and sounded like David's harp.
To the souls of sinners awaiting the Messiah –
He alone was predestined by God to be the Messiah.

To comfort God's Adamites in pains like Nehemiah,
And in lamentation like the prophet Jeremiah,
Over a wicked sinful, and adulterous generation.
To many who were devoid of light or in degradation.

For the Leopards stings sank deep in corruption
As Elohim's plans he hijacked from the generations.
He came not in the manner of he who fell
But of he who created to prepare for his Hell.

Corrupted miscreants worked hard like lunatics
Stumbled, and called him another new heretic.
But he was and is our high and eternal High Priest
Coming from above like a dove to restore the priests.

Who spoke with power and was prophetic
For he made all and could show the way realistic
Who warned many of hypocrisy called yeast
For he alone and deliver men from the Beast.

He was the fullness of Elohim' divine deity.
Who lampooned human unrighteous piety.
To cleanse the Earth needed an ultimate sacrifice
So, His body He offered as was the perfect sacrifice.

His Kingdom was and is to reign for eternity -
Lucifer prince of darkness in his cruelty,
Condemned him Roman hands on the cross;
For His death shameful redeemed us across;

To meet with Elohim, our Merciful Creator,
To meet with Elohim our merciful inventor.
Creation earnestly waits for the rapture
Ever since He ascended to heaven in departure.

Two kingdoms have been on Earth wrestling
History is repetitive with sacred writings.
Terror reigns, kingdoms against kingdoms
For us to also reign, we need divine wisdom.

ACT 1: SCENE 1

[Empyrean Heaven—
Extraterrestrial Kingdom]

(A Gigantic Book of Life THE TORAH is lying on the Big Divine Throne emitting seven different lights like the radiation of the sun and rainbow combined. Before this Throne is a sanctuary)

(Enter other Heavenly Watchers Angels, Archangels, Thrones, Lords, Principalities, Powers, Cherubim, And Seraphim).

(Voice Over by Metatron)

Then appeared a bright light so dazzling.
Rumbling, lightning, fear gripping and baffling.
Silence was everywhere; nothing dared babbling.
Dead and still, every all creatures wondering,
As nothing else was in motion or dared wandering.

Appeared suddenly, a throne with seven blazing lamps
All around it were twenty elders, all white encamped.
On their head, are golden crowns with eternal stamps.
Light from this throne made their crown-like headlamps.
They were peaceful; nothing around them was damped.

The throne was still, and from it, came a Kingly voice
This voice was light for everyone to rejoice.
His form was never seen, nor known at any time
He was the beginning of all things, even time.
Nobody sat on this throne, not even by choice.
Then appeared the Seraphiel, leader of the Seraphim.
Then a procession of seraphim or angelic hosts.
They were magnificent, yet humble to boast.
They had six wings, with burning zeal for Him.

They flew around the throne, yelling King El-Lohim.
Flapping their wings with all reverence and majesty.
A procession of angelic hosts, all white and in dignity
They sang with long trumpets and harps of gold,
Every time they sang praise, we became bold.
Everyone looked younger, never growing old.

(Chorus continues cherubim singing, flapping their six wings,
and flying round and all-round the throne)

CHORUS

Holy, Holy, Holy, our King on high,
To You, our praises ascend to the sky.
You were, You are, and You live evermore,
In worship, our souls find a boundless shore.

In every place, at each sacred hour,
With hearts ablaze, we feel Your power.
Eternal and unchanging, Your glory prevails,
Our devotion to You, our spirits never unfail.

(V.O. by Metatron Continues)

Music from the seraphim dies down,
Everything seemed down or breakdown.
Casting their golden crowns in a vocal range
Twenty-four elders with golden voices so strange
Will sing to the King on the throne invisible.

Though invisible, his presence is visibly invincible
His mighty presence very strongly felt as very visible.
Prostrate to the flood, their forehead will kiss,
They will sing in honor, of the King's bliss;
For He is the King of Kings in all spheres.

ELDERS

Worthy are You, Oh Great King
To receive honor, glory, and power...
You're, above all, all creatures before You sing.
You created all things, and by your power
For Your praise, every creation's duty is to sing.

No creature ever determined Your will
For all You created were in Your perfect will.
You've written Your will in the Torah with a fire quill
You created us in love, in You alone is our being.
You're the Almighty, Your eyes all-seeing.

(V.O. Continues by Metatron, Angel of His Presence, Knower of Secrets)

Clapping envelops the atmosphere.
There is joy everywhere, even in the exosphere.
There is rebirth, even in the air.
The glory is too glorious to behold and bear.
The twenty-four elders are now seated gracefully.

All other angelic hosts stand by in awe, faithfully
Waiting faithfully to worship earnestly,
Admiring the seraphim flap their wings.
Beautiful air quite fresh from their wings
It was an atmosphere of majestic Royalty.

Lucifer, Michael, and Gabriel are Royal,
Made special to remain the King's loyal.
By the throne, they all will parade,
Michael will appear with his mighty blade
Metatron with the scrolls of Good news from Elohim.

Then Gabriel and Lucifer, ready to take orders,
Orders for any mission, even beyond borders.
They will fall prostrate to pledge loyalty,
To Almighty King, who is key to their eternal Royalty
A wonderful privilege to be in his presence.
A wonderful privilege to be in his omnipresence.

(Extraterrestrial Kingdom)

(Chorus continues with the cherubim, singing, flapping
their six wings, and flying around the throne)

CHORUS

Holy, Holy, Holy, Is Our King,
Unto you shall we praise and sing.
Who Was, and is, and lives forever.
We shall worship you wherever and whenever.

ELOHIM

(The book on the throne begins to open and stops on its first page,
the book of Genesis. A radiating powerful voice like a rainbow
from the throne begins speaking).

I am who I am.
I am what I am.
I Am the Ancient of Days.
I Am the Father of All Lights.

I Am the El-Shaddai-The Almighty King.
I Am the Elohim-The Omnipotent King.
I Am the El-Elyon- The Most High King.
I Am El-Olam. The Everlasting King.

I Am the El-Roi-The King Who Sees.
I Am the King of Hosts.
I am Elohim Chayim - The Living God.

I am El Elyon - The Most High God.

(Then twenty-four elders fall before the book on the Throne and worship him who lives forever and ever. They lay their crowns before the throne)

(Chorus Continues, Twenty-Four Elders Singing)

ELDERS

Worthy are You, Oh Great King, so high,
To receive honor, glory, in the sky.
Above all, creation praises Your name,
For You shaped all things, Your power aflame.

No creature altered Your divine intent,
In Your perfect will, all beings were sent.
In the Torah's sacred words, Your wisdom shines,
In love, You formed us, in Your light, we find.

You're the Almighty, with all-seeing sight,
In Your presence, we find eternal light,
The Almighty, with eyes all-seeing, ever-wise,
In adoration and reverence, our voices rise.

ARCHANGELS

(Repeating King Elohim's attributes with a louder male voice like an army ready for war)

You are the El-Shaddai
You are the Elohim
You are the El-Elyon
You are the El-Roi

You are the El-Olam.
You are the Lord of Hosts.
You are Elohim Chayim -

You are El Elyon.

(King Elohim begins to call the names of some of the Royal Guards and their roles in his Kingdom. These three Royal Guards are Michael, Gabriel, and Lucifer)

(The scene fades with the elders and angels praising god).

[Empyrean Heaven — extraterrestrial Kingdom]

(KING ELOHIM begins to call the names of some of the Triumvirate Royal Guards and appoint them to their roles in his Kingdom. These three Royal Guards are Michael, Gabriel, and Lucifer).

ELOHIM

I AM the sovereign King, Immutable,
I created the Earth and water indispensable,
I created the air and fire unquenchable,
I created day and created night irrefutable.

I created the seen and unseen undisputable,
I created light and darkness both mutable
I created the unseen in nine classes indisputable,
I created them in three orders so compatible.

I AM the Sovereign King, Immutable,
I created them all perfect and so indispensable,
Cherubim, Seraphim, and Thrones, all suitable
That all creations bow before me indisputable.

Cherubim, wisdom of my creation and motion,
Seraphim wisdom of creation, fiery motion.
Thrones, wisdom of creation, fixed motion,
My throne bearers, glorious, so imputable.

I AM the sovereign King, Immutable,
I created them all perfect and so indispensable,
Lords, motion with might to conquer or subdue
Powers, motion to my will in full sight or view.

Rulers, motion rulers of the sun, moon, and stars,

Against the evil daring darts, aiming at the stars.
Lords, powers, and rulers, all formidable
I AM the sovereign King, Immutable.

I created them all perfect and so indispensable,
The Earthly and Heavenly realms I made suitable.
Principalities, motion, and rulers of all elements,
They rule with justice without any sentiment.

Arch Angels, motion, and rulers of all creatures,
They rule and govern with invincible features.
Except one man, made or created in my nature -
Angels, the guardian of man, in his frail nature.

Principalities, Arch Angels, and angels are all able.
All by my power, by my word so formidable.
The Heavenly realms shall bear my glory
And the Earthly realms shall embrace my legacy.

(Chorus by the Cherubim, singing, flapping their six wings, and flying round and all around the throne)

CHORUS

Holy, Holy, Holy, our Sovereign King,
To You, our praises and songs we bring.
You were, You are, and forever shall be,
In worship, we find our spirits set free.

In every place, at each sacred time,
With reverence, we lift our voices in rhyme.
Eternal and unchanging, Your glory does ring,
Our devotion to You, our eternal King.

(Chorus Continues, Twenty-Four Elders Singing)

ELDERS

Worthy are You, Oh Great King
To receive honor, glory, and power...
You're, above all, all creatures before You sing.
You created all things, and by your power
For Your praise, every creation's duty is to sing.

No creature ever determined Your will
For all You created were in Your perfect will.
You've written Your will in the Torah with a fire quill
You created us in love, in You alone is our being.
You're the Almighty, Your eyes all-seeing

ELOHIM

Michael, my trusted prince of war.
You shall strike any foe to the core,
Any foe, ungrateful and smarmy -
Commander in chief of my army.

I have braced you a special armor,
To battle and overcome prince of nations
Who stands against my kingdom notions,
Or stand against my Kingdom's reign and motions.

You shall strike evil princes' heels with no emotions
You shall be the solution to many's devotions,
Entangled in darkness, seeking promotions,
Seeking for light, in moments of dark commotions.

(Angelic Hosts and Watchers - Yelling).

Michael! Michael! Michael!

ELOHIM

(Continues)

Gabriel, my trusted royal messenger.

You shall not be an ordinary passenger.
A passenger messenger of my divine will,
To all, I have created with a free mind and will.

To them that heed to your voice while in doom,
Shall obtain mercy, in my presence and Kingdom.
Your voice shall be a trumpet of joy and happiness,
Those that shall heed to your voice's blissfulness.

You will give back hope, to the hopeless
Bring to the downtrodden my good news
Those whose hearts will receive the news
Shall enter my rest, and a life full of my peacefulness.

(Angelic Hosts and Watchers - Yelling).

Gabriel! Gabriel! Gabriel!

ELOHIM

(Continues)

Lucifer, King's light bearer to all,
Beware, not to cause any to fall.
A day shall come, you will stand tall,
Beware of this, it will be your flaw.

It will be a woeful fall, unpleasant at all.
When such a day shall come, beware of gall!
Be wise, not to let it tame your heart,
Your redemption will be extremely hard.

I see the end of things from every beginning,
I am the beginning, in me, all is ever spinning,
I am the end of all, in me, it's always winning,
I created all things perfectly in the beginning.

Without me, you will always go sinning
But with me, in my glory, you go swimming,
My mercy and love are for all without thinning.
I am generous, abounding in all love, twinning.

(Angelic Hosts and Watchers - Yelling)

(V.O. Continues by Metatron).

*Lucifer's heart, like an ice block melted within
In him at creation was wisdom built in.
The Great King Elohim had seen in him a flaw,
Which no one did see in him or saw.*

*Indeed, Lucifer was a host of light
A form of light called wisdom so bright.
Forewarned of his evil pride, but claimed too wise,
Till the daytime will tell of his pride and boast.*

LUCIFER

No, my King, I am and will forever,
Be loyal to your kingship, and will never
Ever let my heart think of evil or clever;
I pledge to be at your service, wherever.

I pledge to do your wish or will, whichever,
I pledge to be at your service whenever,
I pledge to be to your service, whatever,
I pledge to be at your service, whatsoever.

Please, predict not my end to be that of doom,
You've adorned me with beauty and all bloom,
How could I betray you, or dig my own tomb?
If ever, will you permit, let me have a happy tomb.

ELOHIM

I will let the prediction of time speak.
None did I create with a future bleak.
You are all masters of your own fate.
I am immutable; my love will never fade.

(Chorus continues with the cherubim, singing, flapping their six wings, flying around and all around the throne)

CHORUS

Holy, Holy, Holy, Is Our King,
Unto You shall we praise and sing.
Who was, and is, and lives forever.
We shall worship you wherever and whenever.

(V.O. Continues by Metatron).

Mumbling words from an invisible light
Words so gentle, yet stronger than a plight.
There is curiosity in everyone's mind.
Every tongue is tame, all thoughts quarantined.

Nobody knows what will happen next
No host was sage enough to be a suspect.
Every creature stood still and perplexed.
Elohim, a loud radiating voice of light

Like many peals of thunder in full dynamite.
Proceeded from his voice of light, a big ball
Spherical in nature, never seen at all,
The heart of many hosts froze and did crawl.

Then was the birth of something called Earth
Which Elohim called his footstool – the Earth -
From the extraterrestrial came another Kingdom
None of the hosts understood this wisdom.

[EXEUNT
Scene Fades Off]

**[Flashback— 2000 Years
Before The Creation Of The Heavens And Earth]**

(V.O. by Metatron)

Genesis was not the beginning,
Before Genesis was the beginning,
There was another 2,000 years beginning
This was the beginning of all beginnings.

Remember, In the beginning of all, beginnings
There was the WORD in the beginning.
This WORD was God in the beginning
Elohim was this WORD in the beginning.

All things were made by him in the beginning,
Without HIM in the beginning of all beginnings
Nothing was made that was made in the beginning.
In HIM was Life and Light for all in the beginning.

There was a deity, Chaos, a prince of darkness.
Darkness was his delight and deep darkness.
Elohim decided to create another world of light.
For was Life and light was his own delight.

Chaos was unhappy and there was contention.
This contention didn't stop Elohim's intentions,
To create the Heavens and Earth for his pleasure.
Chaos was defeated, then vanished in displeasure.

Elohim then began a master plan for the universe
After creating many worlds and multiverse.
Heavens and Earth is what many are verse.
But the multiverse is complex and diverse.

Before the creation of Heavens and Earth began
Elohim has laid out its foundation and plan.
He himself wrote a book with black fire
An unquenchable fire, also like white fire.

This book of books was called The Torah
In which he swore by his name and aura
His plans, justice, mercy, and redemption
For everything HE was to create at creation.

He forged for himself a Divine Throne of Light
The light was so pure to dissolve even all lights.
On the right side of HIS Throne was Paradise.
When after creating man, was to be imparadised.

To the left of his Throne, he also created Hell
This was a horrible place to think of or tell.
In front of his Throne was a golden sanctuary
It was so Holy that nothing evil or noctuary

Could venture its periphery without indignation.
On this sanctuary was a lamb before the foundation
Who was slained, and also his name boldly written.
Who was to redeem man, but after being smitten.

Before the Heavens and Earth were finally created.
Though he knew his holiness will be desecrated
He vowed not to destroy them in his indignation
But gave everyone a free will and free imagination.

He was to be the supreme judge of all creation,
But mercy and love was to be his pre-occupation.
He then created the heavens, and the watchers
He then created the Earth as a master potter.

Despite all the pre-Genesis wonders of creation,

Man or the angels had no clue or imagination.
As time when on, his plans unfolded gradually
As time went on, his plan unfolded naturally.

Beneath Elohim's throne was a white ball
It looked like snow about to fall.
Snow fell from heaven for hours unknown
It came directly from Elohim's Throne.

This snow became massive in its form
Gradually, this snow was terraformed.
Elohim called it by a divine name—Earth
Chaos prince of darkness invaded the Earth.

(Enter Elohim, as light emanating from a Gigantic Book on this Divine Throne)

(Enter chorus Cherubim singing, flapping their six wings, and flying round and all-round the throne)

CHORUS

Holy, Holy, Holy, Is Our King,
Unto You shall we praise and sing.
Who was, who is, and who lives forever.
We shall worship You wherever and whenever.

ELOHIM

(Day 1 Creation)

Let there be light…
For every creature's delight.
My Spirit will hover around as a knight
Until my will is established, well and right.

(Empyrean Heavens
Extraterrestrial Kingdom)

(Chorus continues with the cherubim, singing, flapping their six wings, flying around, and all the throne).

CHORUS
Holy, Holy, Holy, Is Our King,
Unto You shall we praise and sing.
Who was, and is, and lives forever.
We shall worship You wherever and whenever

(V.O. Continues by Metatron)

So, there was light!
Also there was deep and thick darkness
Darkness or Chaos that made the Earth shapeless,
Even the Earth could not comprehend this.

Part of this darkness was also called night,
There was day, and day was clothed with daylight.
King Elohim also created fire.
Fire to consume and also to purify.

(Chorus continues with the cherubim, singing, flapping their six wings, flying around, and all the throne)

ELDERS
Worthy are You, Oh Great King
To receive honor, glory, and power...
You're, above all, all creatures before You sing.
You created all things, and by your power
For Your praise, every creation's duty is to sing.

No creature ever determined Your will
For all You made, created were in Your perfect will.
You've written Your will in the Torah with a fire quill
You created us in love, in You alone is our being.

You're the Almighty, Your eyes all-seeing.

ELOHIM

(Day 2 Creation)

Let there be a vault between the waters.
To show off my powers and wonders.
To separate water from the kingdom Earth.
So, life on the planet Earth is now birth.

(Empyrean Heavens—
Extraterrestrial Kingdom)

(Chorus continues with the cherubim, singing, flapping
their six wings, flying around, and all the throne).

CHORUS

Holy, Holy, Holy, Is Our King,
Unto you shall we praise and sing.
Who was, and is, and lives forever.
We shall worship you wherever and whenever

(V.O. Continues by Metatron)

So, there was a vault or firmament,
All King Elohim said was permanent.
Under the firmament, were divided waters
He also created creatures under the waters.

ELOHIM

Let the water under the sky be gathered.
So that they are not on Earth slathered.
All the waters are blessed, they are life
By water, man shall live eat and survive.

*(Chorus continues with the cherubim, singing, flapping
their six wings, flying around, and all the throne).*

ELDERS

Worthy are You, Oh Great King
To receive honor, glory, and power...
You're, above all, all creatures before You sing.
You created all things, and by your power
For Your praise, every creation's duty is to sing.

No creature ever determined Your will
For all You made, created were in Your perfect will.
You've written Your will in the Torah with a fire quill
You created us in love, in You alone is our being.
You're the Almighty, Your eyes all-seeing.

(V.O. Continues by Metatron)

*So, the rivers came together in unity
The oceans came together in harmony,
Seas merged together as one community.
Lakes came together in conformity.*

ELOHIM

(Day 3 Creation)

Let the land produce vegetation of all kind.
A breed of diversity, a gift to all mankind.
A new breed, a new creation, and a design.
The Earth is my glory, all to me inclined.

*(Empyrean Heavens—
Extraterrestrial Kingdom)*

*(Chorus continues with the cherubim, singing, flapping
their six wings, flying around, and all the throne).*

CHORUS

Holy, Holy, Holy, Is Our King,
Unto you shall we praise and sing.
Who was, and is, and lives forever.
We shall worship you wherever and whenever.

(V.O. by Metatron Continues)

So, new Earth and land did appear.
Vegetation grew, and so were plant and forest
He created animals such as a dear.
All he created was good, beholding interest.

All was pleasing, nothing so abhorrent,
Some rivers moved with fast and strong torrents.
Animals were in two; they walked as mate,
They were happy, male, and female was their fate.

ELOHIM

(Day 4 Creation)

Let there be lights in the vault of the sky…
For all living creatures and birds to fly.
The stars by night shall shine, and all comply,
The sun by day shall shine, till dusk drops by.

ELDERS

Worthy are You, Oh Great King
To receive honor, glory, and power...
You're, above all, all creatures before You sing.
You created all things, and by your power
For Your praise, every creation's duty is to sing.

No creature ever determined Your will
For all You made, created were in Your perfect will.

You've written Your will in the Torah with a fire quill
You created us in love, in You alone is our being.
You're the Almighty, Your eyes all-seeing.

(V.O. by Metatron Continues)

So, something appeared called the sun
Sparkling like the appearance of His son.
Something so hot, radiating with blazing
A wonder, of the day, always amazing.

It rises cold, gets hot and the set to the east
A light, so faithful that never deceased.
To govern the night, was called the moon
The moon and stars, all learn to commune.

ELOHIM

(Day 5 Creation)

Let lights in the vault of the sky,
Give light to the Earth, a source of new life.
A life without pain, blissful without strife
Let every kind be a community of its ally.

(V.O. by Metatron Continues)

Angelic hosts and watchers were amazed.
There was another wonder for them to gaze
Some did merry, some worship or praise
Others were happy, yet within fazed.

(Chorus continues with the cherubim, singing, flapping
their six wings, flying around, and all the throne).

ELDERS
Worthy are You, Oh Great King

To receive honor, glory, and power...
You're, above all, all creatures before You sing.
You created all things, and by your power
For Your praise, every creation's duty is to sing.

No creature ever determined Your will
For all You made, created were in Your perfect will.
You've written Your will in the Torah with a fire quill
You created us in love, in You alone is our being.
You're the Almighty, Your eyes all-seeing.

ELOHIM

(Day 6 Creation)

Let the Earth bring forth vegetation,
After their kind, there shall be procreation.
Animals of their kind shall by reproduction
Multiply according to the laws of attraction.

(Chorus continues cherubim singing, flapping their six wings, and flying round and all-round the throne)

CHORUS

Holy, Holy, Holy, Is Our King,
Unto You shall we praise and sing.
Who was, who is, and who lives forever.
We shall worship You wherever and whenever.

ELOHIM

(To Michael)

Haste—
Get me some Earth from paradise
To create my own likeness beyond a price.
The one that will rule the Earth forever and rise
To establish justice to be more precise.

To create my own likeness beyond a price.

(Exit Michael, re-enter with a drop of water)

ELOHIM

(To Gabriel)

Haste—
Bring me a drop of water from the sea
To create the ruler the waters and sea
All creatures in all the deep waters
All the oceans, lakes, long or short rivers.

(Exit Gabriel and re-enter with a drop of water)

ELOHIM

(To Lucifer)

Bring me a spark of fire from my holy altar
To create my own likeness that can't be altered.
He shall be the ruler over all angels and creation
 And the works of my hands all at creation.

(Exit Lucifer and re-enter with a spark of fire)

ELOHIM

(To myriads of gathered Angels)

Here I have taken a pop of air
To create my own likeness as an heir.
He shall rule all creatures of the air.
His justice shall be just and fair.

(Chorus continues Cherubim singing, flapping their six wings, and flying round and all-round the throne)

CHORUS

Holy, Holy, Holy, Is Our King,
Unto You shall we praise and sing.
Who was, who is, and who lives forever.
We shall worship You wherever and whenever.

ELOHIM

His name shall be called Adam!
He shall be the first man or human.
To dwell on the new Earth as a leader.
All angels shall bow to him as their ruler.

(Enter Chorus myriads of Angels)

Oh Great King and Mighty Elohim
What is man, thou are mindful of him?
You made him lower than use angels,
But he is clothed in majesty beyond Archangels

We shall bow before him as commanded
We shall bow before him as demanded.
What is man, thou are mindful of him?
You made him lower than use angels,
But he is clothed in majesty beyond Archangels

ELOHIM

(To all myriads of Angels with a loud voice)

To which angel or archangels,
Did I ever say, "You are my son?"
Today, I have become your father?
None in creation, even to the sun.

Chorus by Myriads of Angels

We shall worship him as the begotten

The only son never to be forgotten.
You have made us angels ministering spirits
You are Elohim of all our spirits.

We shall worship him as the begotten
The only son never to be forgotten.
We shall worship him with holy desire
For you have made him a pillar of fire.

ELOHIM

(Day 6 Creation)

Today is my day of rest.
Through creation my power is expressed.
I am over all my creation as omnipresent
For all my creation I will always be present.

(Chorus by Myriads of Angels)

You Are Who You Are
The I AM That I AM.
You Are Who You Are
The I AM What I AM.

You Are Who You Are
The Ancient of Days.
You Are Who You Are
I Am the Father of All Lights.

You Are the El-Shaddai- The Almighty King.
You Are the Elohim-The Omnipotent King.
You Are the El-Elyon- The Most High King.
You Are the El-Roi- The King Who Sees.
You Are the El-Olam. The Everlasting King.
You Are the King of Hosts.

[EXEUNT]

*(V.O. Continues by Metatron, Archangel of His Presence,
Knower of Secrets)*

*Now, a new kingdom had been forged
An addicted mystery, with a strong urge.
The wind blew on the sea, it surged,
Water creatures played and submerged.*

*A mystery to all hosts for them all to master
A puzzle even to Lucifer, the choirmaster.
The three royal and loyal angelic beings
The triumvirate angels went on a mission farseeing.*

*They all departed heaven, all agreeing,
To visit the kingdom Earth for sightseeing.
In the heart of one - Lucifer, the rebel
Grew a heinous and hidden agenda or spell.*

*Though in wonderment, but very unhappy,
He saw Adam as a creature, very sappy.
He was supposed to be the light of the kingdom
He thought only he illuminated the Kingdom.*

*If man was of clay, then he was inferior in wisdom.
He shrugged, thought Elohim was just being dumb.
Why did he even create Adam with such dominion?
With free access to fellowship and communion?*

*Lucifer became envious and very bitter.
He knew Adam was going to be far better.
So, his attention from Elohim will be lesser.
He feared Adam could also be Elohim successor.*

MICHAEL

Hail the King of Kings, King Elohim!
His ways are never indeed predictable.
His wisdom and might are unfathomable.
He created all things, cherubim unlike seraphim.
Hail the King of Kings— King Elohim!

GABRIEL

He's awesome! None compared to him.
Neither powers, angels, cherubim, or seraphim.
His splendor endures from eternity to eternity.
Every luminaries equated to his are vanity.

LUCIFER

I can't believe it—look here!
I can't believe what I see and hear.
Take a quick glimpse before it disappears.
It is worth beyond luminaries of all cheers.

(Talking to Michael and Gabriel, feeling proud that he is one of the most beautiful royals king Elohim had created; one of the most important as well).

LUCIFER

(Continues)

My entire body generates and radiates light.
A light of divine glory to everyone's delight.
I am confident to be the wisest of all in the heavenly.
That's mine thought, it seems quite so apparently.

GABRIEL

It is evident, you are the herald of dawn,
And with such glory, you've been adorned.
The brightest of all the morning stars formed.

None needs to be told about or be informed.

(From an extraterrestrial kingdom, Angels, Archangels, Thrones, Lords, Principalities, Powers, Cherubim, and Seraphim are watching with admiration the wonders of creation)

LUCIFER

You're the preferred of King Elohim
Your bear his name, identity, a true synonym.
He must have a mission for you so special
That one can't know even from his facial.

MICHAEL

We are all exceptional, but different.
There is no need to sound indifferent.
We have taken an allegiance to be belligerent.
We have one king; we will live to defend.

GABRIEL

It should not be of any concern
The King loves us equally, it is certain.
We must not think otherwise to err.
Everything he does it good and fair.

LUCIFER

It was just a thought, my perception.
We do not have the same conception.
Let's give it a second thought or reflection
We have seen what he has done from inception.

(Lucifer is not happy. he feels that since he does not have the name of king Elohim added to his name from creation, king Elohim indeed prefers other royal guards than him).

MICHAEL

Beware of jokes, that lead to heinous curiosity.
Wrong jokes are sometimes roots for animosity.
We were all created and loved with equality.
Beware, get rid of any impending jealousy.

LUCIFER
(Flashback)

Lucifer, King's light bearer to all,
Beware, not to cause any to fall.
A day shall come, you will stand tall,
Beware of this, it will be your flaw.

GABRIEL
Don't allow boredom to be your guest,
I do think you're bored, it's just a guess!
Let not silly jokes be or taint your noblesse,
For sure, we all know we are above all blessed.

LUCIFER
(Looking at the kingdom Earth, vegetation, and animals, lucifer notices they reproduce only after their kind. Lucifer is really amazed and wants to know more).

Let's get closer—
I guess I have been a poser!
Everything here reproduces only after its kind.
This is amazingly amazing to my mind.
This is imaginary, too real to believe or find!

(Animals talking and grazing. Animals of all kinds or their own species are paired in twos, males, and females).

GABRIEL
It does beseem light begets light—
Darkness begets darkness alike, nights begets night.

The hidden wisdom of Creation,
Unknown to us all in its formation.

LUCIFER

(Talking To Himself).

If light begets light.
Then I can beget other lights.
If I am light, shouldn't I be a king or god?
A stronger king who can rule with a rod?

(Enter Elohim's voice to Lucifer as a flashback)

It will be a woeful fall, unpleasant at all.
When such a day shall come, beware of gall!
Be wise, not to let it tame your heart,
Your redemption will be extremely hard.

GABRIEL

Lucifer, be watchful and be mindful
I perceive your thoughts are already full.
Your thought can speak louder in heaven.
Let is not become a contentious leaven.

MICHAEL

We were all created with glorious perfection
None were created with any imperfection.
We have a free will, which can lead to defection.
We have a free will, which can lead to rejection.

LUCIFER

I have a free will, but is my will free?
I want to be as free as the wind or bee.
I don't need a king to whom I'll bow to my knees.
I know you don't support; do we all agree?

(Enter Elohim's voice to Lucifer as flashback)

I see the end of things from every beginning,
I am the beginning, in me, all is ever spinning,
I am the end of all, in me, it's always winning,
I created all things perfect in the beginning.

GABRIEL

Do not question the King's authority,
None can compete with his superiority.
He is out king, our royal majesty,
I advise you to get rid of this malignity.

LUCIFER

Only the brave can talk back to the King,
You are a coward if you can't say anything.
Can't you learn to see things and think?
If you can think of anything, then you stink!

MICHAEL

(Pulling his sword for a fight, but Gabriel stops Michael).

You can be a fool, but don't be foolish,
Your pride will soon be defeated or will vanish.
Without any mercy, you will perish in anguish,
My loyalty to the King will never diminish.

GABRIEL

Let's halt this senseless argument.
We did not come on Earth for entertainment
We ought to be happy or in merriment.
King Elohim is right with his wit and judgement.

LUCIFER

None of you have any aspiration
That's why you don't have any inspiration.

I will be king one day with great admiration.
You will serve me under administration.

(Enter Elohim's voice to Lucifer as flashback)

Without me, you will always go sinning
But with me, in my glory, you go swimming,
My mercy and love are for all without thinning.
I am generous, abounding in all love, twinning.

MICHAEL

Your doom is pending, I see the damnation.
Your doom is pending, I see the condemnation.
You were created with utmost perfection,
Evil has eaten your heart and intellection.

LUCIFER

Nothing wrong with my intellection
Only the weak speak of subjection.
You think it is bowing by affection.
All kings know of the word "disaffection."

MICHAEL

Your days are numbered!
You can't win alone, you're outnumbered.
Wake up from hallucinations and slumber
Make peace within and finally surrender.

LUCIFER

Michael, I have long given myself peace
Let your counsel of doom cease.
Are you jealous that I seek to increase?
I can see, and I know your malice and caprice.

(Enter Elohim's voice to Lucifer as a flashback)

Lucifer, King's light bearer to all,
Beware, not to cause any to fall.
A day shall come, you will stand tall,
Beware of this, it will be your flaw.

It will be a woeful fall, unpleasant at all.
When such a day shall come, beware of gall!
Be wise, not to let it tame your heart,
Your redemption will be extremely hard.

(Trumpets from the upper heaven begin to sound).

LUCIFER

(Laughter).

(The Three Royal Guards fly back to the heavens. Lucifer is thoughtful and keeps thinking that he's a demi-god and next in the lines of the kings to King Elohim since he carries a glory higher than any other royal host).

[EXEUNT]

**[Empyrean Heaven —
Extraterrestrial Kingdom]**

(V.O. by Metatron Continues)

Luminaries have been formed or created,
What other hosts least expected.
Five days after the Earth or its creation
King Elohim hosted a heavenly operation.

With his son, Christ of all creation and mankind,
It is a sacred counsel about the fate of humankind.
The Seraphim are allowed to this sacred meeting
There are twelve other thrones with golden seating.

On these thrones seats, are twelve shining crowns
One can hear melodious voices producing sounds.
The seraphim flapping their wings in reverence
Singing, "Holy, Holy to our king" as a reference.

(Empyrean Heavens— Extraterrestrial Kingdom)

(Chorus continues with the cherubim, singing, flapping
their six wings, flying around, and all the throne)

CHORUS
Holy, Holy, Holy, our voices raise,
In awe of your glory, we offer our praise.
You were, you are, and forever shall be,
In your presence, we find eternity's key.

Majestic King, in your splendor we find,
A love that's unending, infinitely kind.
With every breath, our worship we bring,

To the Holy, Holy, Holy, our eternal King.

(V.O. by Metatron Continues)

King Elohim—
From the throne is a strong radiation
From this radiation, a strong utterance of oration.
This is the presence of King Elohim, his majesty.
A king never seen, but known for his Majesty.

Now appears his son, the Lord of all Lords.
He is next to the King, and works in one accord.
No heavenly host knows about him or his record.
But he is the King's pride, the savior
Creator of all hosts, and man in his nature.

CHRIST

Creation looks impeccable,
But with free will they are peccable.
Our love for humanity remains stable
And our gifts to mankind remain irrevocable.

ELOHIM

Indeed, with free will, creation is peccable,
Other creatures will be more susceptible.
There is a master plan if they really fumble.
Creation is still tender, immature, and unstable.

CHRIST

A master plan is very imperative,
To save those that fall by means explorative.
Curiosity is a flaw for some, very tentative,
By which they can fall for anything attractive.

ELOHIM

Creation has yet to come to a mature age,

We must extend our kingship lineage.
Where man will be made in our image,
The Kingdom Earth will be his stage.

CHRIST

What is the plan for man's creation?
What's his role amidst other creation?
Would he be created in a particular location?
Where he will rule over kingdoms or nations?

ELOHIM

Eden will be his place of creation -
We will watch his behavior or mutation.
Man was in my mind before the foundation,
And the creation of the Earth and all nations.

CHRIST

If made in our image and likeness,
He should also be clothed with meekness.
A divine virtue, not any form of weakness -
He's our image, exceptional in uniqueness.

ELOHIM

You're perfectly right and alright,
He will be created with a scepter to smite.
He will be set on Zion of great height
He will be to other creatures their light.

CHRIST

Light to others if he remains the light,
By which he will prevail as his birthright.
He must be ready to put up a good fight
Against the evil soon to appear by his side.

ELOHIM

Yes —

One of the created luminaries
Will soon gather other revolutionaries.
Those that willfully become our adversaries,
Will have to follow the same fate or miseries.

CHRIST

Every rebellion is an evil seed for no reward,
For any creation in rebellion or disaccord.
This should be their insurrection record,
Michael must also ready his sword.

ELOHIM

Michael is my faithful servant
His reaction to avenge is very fervent.
All this while, he has been observant
With his sword, he will defeat all insurgents.

CHRIST

I am glad we'd created the abyss,
For all who maliciously align amiss.
Others will learn from this premise.
That rebellion can lead to one's demise.

ELOHIM

I created them out of love and not hate
I am still patient and compassionate.
I have given him time to think or ruminate.
Before his lust consumes him or dominates.

CHRIST

Should we summon him for a hearing?
To uncover his pretense as if god-fearing?
His attitude is dangerous, not endearing,
Others will falter, not knowing they're erring.

ELOHIM

My constitution is built into every creation
I taught them my law during formation.
They have a conscience for direction
The have my laws for divine correction.

CHRIST

We have given every creation options
They must be wise, and exercise caution.
Man must be warned not to pay attention
His fall will abort our kingdom extension.

(Extraterrestrial Kingdom)

*(Chorus continues cherubim singing, flapping their six wings,
and flying round and all-round the throne)*

CHORUS

Holy, Holy, Holy, our voices we raise,
To You, O King, we offer our praise.
Who was, who is, and lives forever,
In Your presence, our bonds we sever.

We shall worship You, wherever we roam,
In every place, You make Your home.
With hearts full of gratitude, we sing,
To our eternal King, our praises we bring.

Your glory shines from age to age,
In reverence, our hearts engage.
Holy, Holy, Holy, we adore Your name,
In endless worship, we remain the same.

(V.O. by Metatron Continues)

*Birds were created to fly,
They were given wings to go very high.*

Waters were created for the fish
To swim with leisure as they all wish.

Other water monsters were the whales
A sea monster, faster than all snails;
They were blessed with the bliss to multiply
But there were laws they must comply.

(Chorus continues with the cherubim, singing, flapping
their six wings, flying around, and all the throne).

ELDERS

Worthy are You, Oh Great King, above all,
To receive honor, glory, and power, at Your call.
Every creature before You joins in the song,
You created all things, where we all belong.

For Your praise, every creation's duty is to sing,
In harmonious praise, let Your praises ring.
No creature can determine Your divine will,
In Your perfect plan, all things find their skill.

You've inscribed Your will in the Torah's sacred line,
With a fiery quill, Your wisdom does shine.
In love, You formed us, our existence You're seeing,
You're the Almighty, with eyes ever-seeing.

[EXEUNT]

[Extraterrestrial Kingdom]

(V.O. by Metatron Continues)

Before the rise of a new dawn or morning
The sixth day, everything was adorning.
Michael and Gabriel summon all heavenly hosts
With a trumpet, rallying all host from their posts.

All hosts were gathered, like in a Roman Circus Maximus
They were anxious, but at the same time equanimous.
They were all gathered around Elohim's throne
Some of the hosts were identical, like a clone.

There were flashlights, thunder, and rumbling,
Except for one, angry within, and grumbling.
None knew what to expect, some were mumbling
Many were the hosts of light, all outnumbering.

Everywhere lit in glory, in a way so extraordinary
What was unfolding before all wasn't ordinary.
Yet one among them in a fit of darkness
Nursing evil plans to obstruct the great light.

(Day 6 of Creation)

(Extraterrestrial Kingdom)

(Chorus continues with the cherubim, singing, flapping
their six wings, flying around, and all the throne).

CHORUS
Holy, Holy, Holy, our voices we raise,
To our King, we offer heartfelt praise.

Who was, and is, and lives forevermore,
In Your presence, our souls do adore.

We shall worship You, wherever we stand,
In every moment, at Your command.
With reverence and love, our voices we lend,
To the eternal King, our praises ascend.

ELOHIM

Light begets light.
Darkness begets darkness,
In darkness, there is happiness.
In light, there is much delight.

Let the beast be for the beast
Let them multiply, and increase.
Let them have dominion, as priests.

(Chorus Continues, Twenty-Four Elders Singing).

ELDERS

Worthy are You, Oh Great King, on high,
To receive honor, glory, and power, we comply.
Above all, creatures before You gladly sing,
You created all things, by Your mighty wing.

For Your praise, every creation's voice shall ring,
In harmonious chorus, our gratitude we bring.
No creature can alter Your divine will,
In Your perfect purpose, all is fulfilled.

Inscribed in the Torah with a fiery quill,
Your wisdom and love, our spirits thrill.
In You alone, our existence finds its meaning,
You're the Almighty, with eyes all-seeing.

CHORUS

Holy, Holy, Holy, our voices we raise,
To our King, we offer reverent praise.
Who was, and is, and lives forevermore,
In Your presence, our spirits do adore.

We shall worship You, wherever we stand,
In every moment, at Your command.
With hearts full of love, our voices we lend,
To the eternal King, our praises ascend.

ELOHIM

Let's make man in our likeness and image.
Let him be fruitful through his lineage.
Let him multiply and grace with age
Let him replenish the entire Earth as his stage.

Let him subdue all kingdoms, in love or rage
Many years shall he rule till the end of his age.
Let him have dominion all over all heavenly hosts;
He is my express image, on whom I can boast.

All heavenly hosts must go prostrate before him
He is my image, the likeness of Elohim.
In him, I am well pleased, as the new light;
A light to shine so bright, day and night.

He shall be called Adam; he shall sit on high
And I shall lift him up on the Earth so high,
His kingdom shall know no end
From his loins, generations shall descend.

(Chorus continues with the cherubim, singing, flapping their six wings, flying around, and all the throne).

ELDERS

Worthy are You, Oh Great King, on high,
To receive honor, glory, and power, we testify.
Above all, creatures before You humbly sing,
You created all things, by Your sovereign wing.

For Your praise, every creation's voice does ring,
In harmonious devotion, our gratitude we bring.
No creature can alter Your divine will,
In Your perfect purpose, all is fulfilled.

Inscribed in the Torah with a fiery quill,
Your wisdom and love, our hearts fulfill.
In You alone, our existence finds its meaning,
You're the Almighty, with eyes ever-seeing.

ELOHIM

I created him with my bare hands,
I have given him dominion on all lands.
He is my image, he is a microcosm
I am the eternal King, a macrocosm.

He has the scepter to rule the world in miniature
All must bow to him, despite your nature.
His hair is the number of trees on Earth
His tears are the number of all rivers on Earth.

His mouth is to all the oceans on Earth.
The world is spherical as his eyeball
Oceans encircling the Earth, even small
Represent Adam and the white of his eye.
The dry land is the Iris of his eye.

(Chorus continues with the cherubim, singing, flapping their six wings, flying around, and all the throne).

CHORUS

Holy, Holy, Holy, our voices we raise,
To our King, we offer reverent praise.
Who was, and is, and lives forevermore,
In Your presence, our spirits adore.

We shall worship You, wherever we tread,
In every moment, with reverence widespread.
With grateful hearts, our voices we bring,
To the eternal King, our praises we sing.

ELOHIM

He is more than a mere image or template
Of the Earth as we can contemplate.
He embodies all angelic beings or host
He has a free will, an intellect utmost.

Which makes him superior to all angels,
They can eat, drink, and even propagate
Angels don't, they were created to cooperate.
Man in all his glory will die like any beast.

If he chooses to sin like a senseless beast,
Only through death shall he be released -
Released from his mortal body into immortality.
He is both Earth and heaven in glory and unity.

So, the man called Adam was created
From Elohim alone, much debated.
He was of his own kind but all alone
He was Elohim's replica or clone.

Such a creature was never seen and known
Of all the angelic hosts, it was a strange creation.
Strange image, from Elohim's imagination.
He was made and created in Elohim's likeness

All he created was good, but man has no happiness
Man needed someone to seal his fate,
Then, Elohim created him a helper or mate.
They grew together, and later became intimate.

They were also blessed, and given dominion.
Dominion over the sea, waters as a champion.
Adam had the blessing, was put in Eden,
No place as beautiful as the Gulf of Aden.

The trees bore fruits for Adam to eat,
They were all good, tasty, and sweet.
Roots shot out from under the Earth
Still for Adam's food, his all on the Earth.

ELDERS

Worthy are You, Oh Great King, divine,
To receive honor, glory, in Your light we shine.
Above all, creatures before You we bring,
You created all things, under Your sovereign wing.

For Your praise, every creation's voices ring,
In harmonious worship, Your praises we sing.
No creature can alter Your eternal will,

In Your perfect design, all finds fulfillment still.

Inscribed in the Torah with a fiery quill,
Your wisdom and love, our hearts fulfill.
In You alone, our existence finds its meaning,
You're the Almighty, with eyes ever-seeing.

ELOHIM

I am who I am.
I am what I am.
I Am the Ancient of Days.
I Am the Father of All Lights.

I Am the El-Shaddai-The Almighty King.
I Am the Elohim-The Omnipotent King.
I Am the El-Elyon- The Most High King.
I Am El-Olam.The Everlasting King.

I Am the El-Roi-The King Who Sees.
I Am the King of Hosts.
I am Elohim Chayim - The Living God.
I am El Elyon - The Most High God.

(Royal angelic hosts, watchers celebrating and chanting a song of worship. Lucifer begins to develop resentment against king Elohim and Adam).

ELOHIM
(Calling Lucifer, Lucifer comes forward).

I entrust you to keep him out of danger
You were created as his messenger.
I created you in splendor, a smokeless fire.
You must watch out of your desire.

(Lucifer, bowing down before King Elohim in false humility and pretenses).

ELOHIM

I have given you godly wisdom
Also, a free will to reign in my kingdom.
You know my ways, the ways of light.
Guide Adam, let his light remain as a flashlight.

(Extraterrestrial Kingdom)

(Chorus continues with the Cherubim, singing, flapping their six wings, flying around, and all the throne).

CHORUS

Holy, Holy, Holy, Is Our King,
Unto you shall we praise and sing.
Who was, and is, and lives forever.
We shall worship you wherever and whenever.

(Day 7 of Creation)

ELOHIM

My word is a sharper-edged sword.
Of all creation, my word is Lord.
Let life begin, I must retire to rest.
My creation is sanctified and blest.

I Am who I am.
I Am Elohim -
I Am the Ancient of Days.
I Am the Father of All Lights.

I Am the El-Shaddai-The Almighty King.
I Am the Elohim-The Omnipotent King.
I Am the El-Elyon- The Most High King.

I Am El-Olam. The Everlasting King.

I Am the El-Roi - The King Who Sees.
I Am the King of Hosts.
I am Elohim Chayim - The Living God.
I am El Elyon - The Most High God.

(Chorus Continues, Twenty-Four Elders Singing).

ELDERS

Worthy are You, Oh Great King, on high,
To receive honor, glory, and power, we testify.
Above all, creatures before You gladly sing,
You created all things, by Your sovereign wing.

For Your praise, every creation's voice does ring,
In harmonious devotion, our gratitude we bring.
No creature can alter Your eternal will,
In Your perfect purpose, all is fulfilled.

Inscribed in the Torah with a fiery quill,
Your wisdom and love, our hearts fulfill.
In You alone, our existence finds its meaning,
You're the Almighty, with eyes ever-seeing.

[EXEUNT]

[THE SCENE FADES OUT]

[Extraterrestrial Kingdom]

(V.O. by Metatron Continues)

Lucifer finally was truly unhappy,
He became very insidious and snappy.
What relationship was fire and clay?
His thoughts were unstable and did sway.

Adam surpassed him in glory and power
This made him enraged as he did ponder.
His countenance was consumed with bitterness
For desired to be above all the greatest.

Now, before him were two great foes.
He hated both Elohim and Adam in woes.
Deep in his heart were fits of frustration
For man, made of dust placed far higher than him.

Unfortunately, he was the weakness of all,
Thought he desired revenge to cause Adam's fall.
He was not powerful, but crafty to seek revenge
But sooner or later, he still planned to avenge.

Then he will get unusually busy
Fomenting evil plans and corrupting many,
No more punctual as chief musician
And so the glory of Seraphim and Cherubim.

LUCIFER

(To Himself)

I must discover for myself this secret,

In Elohim's mind, it's kept, truly discreet.
He crafted me with woes and misfortune's art,
While other celestial beings find a gentler start.

With determination, I'll seek the truth untold,
In the cosmic design, my destiny unfolds.
For though my path seems shadowed and obscure,
I'll find my purpose, of that I'm sure.

(Enter Elohim's voice to Lucifer as a flashback)

Lucifer, King's light bearer to all,
Beware, not to cause any to fall.
A day shall come, you will stand tall,
Beware of this, it will be your flaw.

LUCIFER

(Continues to himself)

What sacred truth could He be guarding in silence,
That King Elohim deems to be sacred and intense?
For His knowledge alone, He chose to hold the key,
In reverent silence, His wisdom does decree.

No reason He saw, to share with His kind,
In solemn silence, His secret did bind.
Mysteries concealed, in His eternal grace,
Only within His heart, that sacred place.

(Enter Elohim's voice to Lucifer as a flashback)

It will be a woeful fall, unpleasant at all.
When such a day shall come, beware of gall!
Be wise, not to let it tame your heart,
Your redemption will be extremely hard.

LUCIFER

(Continues)

Adam is now my deadly rival for eternity
I must render Elohim's hope turn to vanity.
I was created first and existed before him
Why must he be the one chosen by Elohim?

(Repeating to himself in a bitter resentment)

Adam, my rival, in this eternal strife,
I seek to thwart Elohim's plan for life.
I existed first, before his earthly birth,
Yet Elohim chose him, the one of earthly worth.

(Enter Elohim's voice to Lucifer as a flashback)

I see the end of things from every beginning,
I am the beginning, in me, all is ever spinning,
I am the end of all, in me, it's always winning,
I created all things perfect in the beginning.

LUCIFER

(Continues)

I will crush you Adam to dust and rust,
You've stolen my love, glory, and trust.
From this dust you were created –
There you must return, not to Heaven.

ELOHIM

(Voice from the throne calling).

(Extraterrestrial Kingdom)

(Chorus continues with the cherubim, singing, flapping their six wings, flying around, and all the throne).

CHORUS

Holy, Holy, Holy, we lift our voices high,
To our Sovereign, we give our worship, nigh.
Who once was, still is, and forevermore,
In Your presence, our spirits deeply adore.

We'll adore You always, wherever we may be,
In every instant, following Your decree.
With hearts full of affection, our voices shall ring,
To the everlasting Monarch, our praises we'll sing.

(Enter Lucifer before the throne, bowing in reference).

ELOHIM

Why is your countenance fallen?
Why is your heart suddenly swollen?
Swollen with pride and disillusionment?
I am compassionate and slow in judgment.

LUCIFER

Gabriel and Michael,
Are they the talebearer for this report?
Indeed my heart is sad and wrought.
Why am I dragged before this court?

ELOHIM

I am omnipotent and omniscient.
I am omnipotent and prospicient.
I am the supreme King and creator.
You were created, I am the ultimate inventor.

Should clay at the mercy of his potter
Argue with him, whatever the matter?

Should a form of existence done by me
Question another form of existence by me?

LUCIFER

My King, You're Sovereign, we all know,
I can't keep this to myself again alone.
I was created with a smokeless fire.
Fire to clay is superior to admire.

ELOHIM

What then is your predicament,
Which makes your heart insolent?
Don't you understand fire or clay?
What darkness covers that you see not clear?

LUCIFER

My King,
All is not clear; fire makes me superior
Adam is made of clay, and so is inferior.
I was created first; I was long in existence.
He needs to serve me, just as I bow in your presence

ELOHIM

You were created first, but he pre-existed.
Your heart was pure, but now conceited.
Fire is superior to clay, but not in my image.
Adam is created in my image for my lineage.

LUCIFER

Aren't we part of the lineage?
What lineage is Adam, a patrilineage?
Justice here is twisted and very unfair
Our glory is not in any way to his compared.

ELOHIM

All created hosts are part of my lineage

No matter when they were created or age.
Amongst them, who else has twelve wings?
You are the only one among other things.

LUCIFER

My King,
Are my wings a measurement of honor?
Adam does not have any wing to his honor
But he is clothed with more glory and power
This means you have made me a little lower.

ELOHIM

Your heart is full of iniquity
You don't seem contented with your beauty.
I am a king full of mercy and tranquility.
Mend your heart, get rid of sin and vanity.

I have given you enough time to repent
Not to fall into damnation and later lament.
My Kingdom and power has no end
But my temper and mercies surely has an end.

LUCIFER

My King, you are the Almighty,
I know your mercy endures forever.
I have a request, if it might be clever,
An exemption from prostrating to Adam -

ELOHIM

I still trust you are of a good mind,
Your mission to Adam has been assigned.
Attending to him you were designed,
Your request is unfortunately is denied.

Love Adam just as I loved you all
Make nothing else to be your love or idol.

Teach Adam just as I have been your mentor
I am your King, your omnipotent creator.

Everyone will have their own reward
But your free will must merit this award.
Everyone I have ever made carry a purpose
Mine own shall not live without purpose.

(Chorus Continues, Twenty-Four Elders Singing).

ELDERS

Worthy are You, Oh Great King
To receive honor, glory, and power...
You're, above all, all creatures before You sing.
You created all things, and by your power
For Your praise, every creation's duty is to sing.

No creature ever determined Your will
For all You made, created were in Your perfect will.
You've written Your will in the Torah with a fire quill
You created us in love, in You alone is our being.
You're the Almighty, Your eyes all-seeing.

[EXIT
Lucifer To Adam]

[In the Garden of Eden]

(Enter Lucifer as a spirit entity).

LUCIFER
(Calling Adam in a persuasive way)

Adam—

(Suddenly a cloudy spiritual portal mirror with the colors of the rainbow or aura appears before Adam. he can see and communicate with Lucifer).

ADAM
Who are you?

LUCIFER
I am Lucifer—
We serve the same Sovereign King
The creator of both visible and invisible things.
I am here to have us talk and think.

ADAM
What are we to talk or think about?
This is my first time seeing you without
Since I began to explore Eden throughout,
I might be wrong, but clear my doubt!

LUCIFER
Obviously, you are not wrong.
The story of our existence is very long.
I pre-existed before you were formed.
You were Earth before being transformed.

ADAM

You called my name; how did you know?
Did you know me in pre-existence, though
I don't seem to know you anywhere
I am just cautious not to err.

LUCIFER

You're right to be cautious not err
King Elohim assigned me to be here.
To help you understand the other Kingdom
Despite the fact that he has given you wisdom.

ADAM

Are there other Kingdoms somewhere?
Are they like the Earth and sphere?
I would much like to learn other things
My kingdom Earth, I know all things.

LUCIFER

Your name Adam—
King Elohim created in all seven heavens.
Each heaven, is so distinct and unique.
Creation was made perfect to its peak.

ADAM

Seven heavens!
Does King Elohim need all this?
Shouldn't one suffice for his bliss?
Well—I'll be glad to hear more please.

LUCIFER

First heaven this is the Earth you see around
Where the other animals are found.
It is the bases for all human life
With all, it takes for a man to survive.

ADAM

What of the second heaven?

LUCIFER

The second heaven—firmament
The second heaven is for other planets
The Earth is the fifth largest planets.
Third from the sun, where life is possible
Other planets, life isn't yet possible.

ADAM

Do spirit beings survive on other planets?
If life is not possible on this other planet,
I guess I will one day visit these planets
And explore the beauty of Elohim's works.

LUCIFER

(Laughing).

In your nature are all the planets
You are the master of all the planets.
You were created in their image
And in Elohim's likeness for his lineage.

ADAM

What of the third heaven?

LUCIFER

The third heaven — Shekinah *(Clouds)*
Manna — sacred for food the saints is made.

ADAM

What of the fourth heaven?

LUCIFER

The fourth heaven—

The celestial Jerusalem

ADAM

What of the angels,
Wherein heaven do they dwell?

LUCIFER

In the fifth haven, some reside.
They praise the King and stand by his side.
They praise by night, and by day
He only accepts man's praises that come his way.
Some pull the King's chariot when he rides.

ADAM

How many angels are there?
Are they male and female or a pair?
Do they reproduce after their kind,
Just it is with all mankind?

LUCIFER

We are many, we are unaccountable
Everyone by his order to be accountable;
We are of three orders
Each of the orders have its leaders.

ADAM

Which are the orders?

LUCIFER

The Highest Orders
Seraphim
Cherubim
Thrones

ADAM

Interesting… any other order?

LUCIFER

Middle Orders
> Dominions
> Virtues
> Powers

ADAM

Waooooo, Is that all?

LUCIFER

Lowest Orders
> Principalities
> Archangels
> Angels

ADAM

What then of the sixth heaven?

LUCIFER

The sixth—residence
This is for all trials and visitations
From here, angels are on missions
To the planet Earth, and give revelations.

King Elohim stores snow, poisonous smoke,
Hailstorms, and thunder that can cause a stroke.
Its chamber doors are fire, controlled by Metatron
Who stores the graces and powers of the Almighty.

ADAM

Finally,
What's the seventh heaven?

LUCIFER

The seventh heaven— Highest Heaven
This is the highest of all heavens

Is supreme of all heavenly haven.
A place of extraordinary beauty and peace.

The abode of good, justice, pious souls,
It is the seat of the throne of Elohim.
Spirits of all unborn children or generations
From here, God can show mercy to all creation.

(Extraterrestrial Kingdom)

(Chorus by the cherubim continues, singing, flapping their six wings, and flying round and all-round the throne)

CHORUS

Holy, Holy, Holy, Is Our King,
Unto you shall we praise and sing.
Who was, and is, and lives forever.
We shall worship you wherever and whenever

(Chorus Continues, Twenty-Four elders singing).

ELDERS

Worthy are You, Oh Great King
To receive honor, glory, and power...
You're, above all, all creatures before You sing.
You created all things, and by your power
For Your praise, every creation's duty is to sing.

No creature ever determined Your will
For all You made, created were in Your perfect will.
You've written Your will in the Torah with a fire quill
You created us in love, in You alone is our being.
You're the Almighty, Your eyes all-seeing.

(Michael and Gabriel sounding a trumpet call).

(Exit Lucifer back to heaven).

ACT 2: SCENE 3

**[Empyrean Heaven —
Extraterrestrial Kingdom]**

(V.O. by Metatron Continues)

*Adam was left alone in the Garden
King Elohim put him in Eden.
He gave names to all the animals,
He knew all animals and mammals.*

*They came to him males and females,
He gave them their names, even the whales.
Adam had one problem, he was lonely
Though adorn in Elohim's glory, he was lonely.*

*Lilith was his first made companion
But it was not a long-lasting union.
Lilith was very beautiful, created from dust,
She was created of the same substance dust.*

*She made herself equal to Adam, not subordinate
Adam's soul was grieved, his joy did abate.
She claimed equal rights based on same origin
King Elohim was not happy for this rebellious sin.*

*From the garden of Eden, she was self-banished
She was self-banished; into the air she did vanish.
Adam complained to Elohim about her character
Elohim sent three angels; she was bound with a fetter.*

*Elohim in his plan never ever made equal
Any being for his unique purpose so was woman,
She was found near the Red Sea, her fate decided
She was even considered have demons, misguided.*

CHORUS

Holy, Holy, Holy, Is Our King,
Unto you shall we praise and sing.
Who was, and is, and lives forever.
We shall worship you wherever and whenever

ELOHIM

Adam looks somehow happy,
But his face is burnt out and shabby.
All animals come to him male and female
He might need one of his kind, not a she-male.
As insubordinate as Lilith—

CHRIST

Definitely, he does need a helpmate
With whom he can be a soul-mate.
With whom he can as well mate
A soul mate for him to mate and be intimate.

ELOHIM

Adam was made from dust
Let's wait to create his mate at dusk.
A mate in whom he will find happiness
Not a mate who will give him bitterness.

CHRIST

It can only be a mate of his kind.
A mate taken from his rib so defined.
Light begets light, so must Adam
He must beget his belle dame.

ELOHIM

We shall cause him to fall asleep,
We'll create him a helpmate from his rib.
A mate that will not cause him to weep,
A mate of his pleasure, even in his sleep.

(Chorus Continues, Twenty-Four Elders Singing)

ELDERS

Worthy are You, Oh Great King
To receive honor, glory, and power...
You're, above all, all creatures before You sing.
You created all things, and by your power
For Your praise, every creation's duty is to sing.

No creature ever determined Your will
For all You made, created were in Your perfect will.
You've written Your will in the Torah with a fire quill
You created us in love, in You alone is our being.
You're the Almighty, Your eyes all-seeing.

ELOHIM

We can't make her from Adam's head
She might be arrogant to think ahead.
We can't create her from Adam's eyes
She might develop them to wanton eyes

We can't create her from Adam's ears
She can be an eavesdropper using her tears.
We can't create her from Adam's neck
She can become insolent to Adam her neck.

We can't create her from Adam's mouth
She can be become chatterer in and out
We cannot create her from Adam's heart
She can become envious wanting to be smart.

We can't create her from Adam's hand
She can become a meddler or even wrestler.
We can't create her from Adam's foot
She can become a gadabout enticed by foot.

We can't create her from Adam's Head
She will fight to become greater than the Head.
We shall create her from Adam rib, by his chest
So that she can be righteous and chaste.

CHRIST

Woman—Womb of the man
Must be created with care for Adam.
Her creation is much complicated
More than of any creation ever created.

ELOHIM

She is designed for childbearing
She needs extra intelligence for caring.
Her body must be soft, to attract Adam for sex,
That's why their desires are somehow complex.

CHRIST

Adam must go for his missing rib,
Seeking Eve his wife in marriage
For this reason, he leaves and be engaged.
For the two shall be one flesh and rib.

(Loud Trumpet Sounds).

(Extraterrestrial Kingdom)

(Enter Other Celestial Hosts Angels, Archangels, Thrones, Lords, Principalities, Powers, Cherubim, And Seraphim).

(Chorus continues with the cherubim, singing, flapping their six wings, flying around, and all the throne).

CHORUS

Holy, Holy, Holy, divine and pure,
Our adoration, forever shall endure.
From ages past to the endless yonder,
In Your presence, our hearts grow fonder.

With unwavering faith, our voices raise,
In every moment, we offer heartfelt praise.
To the everlasting King, our souls align,
In worship and love, forever we'll entwine.

(V.O. by Metatron Continues)

In the presence of all creation
Some of which were in awe or trepidation,
King Elohim stretched his hand toward Adam
For it was time to execute settlement for Adam.

A white mist like a wind blew toward Eden
Where Adam was sitting alone in the Garden.
He yawned, then fell asleep as though dead;
Creation looked terrified and some afraid.

Appeared a sudden beam, like a laser light
Creation watched steadily without insight
As it pointed at Adam's side only, for a rib;
For good breath only comes out of the rib.

Alas! Another Adam's mate was created
She was naked, not ashamed nor conceited.
Adam called her Ishah—woman!
Adam was called Ish—husband

(An uproar like that of an army at war).

(Chorus Continues, Twenty-Four Elders Singing)

ELDERS

Worthy are You, Oh Great King so high,
To receive honor, glory, and power, we magnify.
Above all beings, all creation's voices ring,
You, the Creator, by Your mighty power, bring

Every creature to sing, in harmonious choir,
In praise of Your name, hearts set on fire.
Your perfect will, none can ever thwart or chill,
In the Torah's words, Your wisdom does distill.

In love, You crafted us, in Your image, we're formed,
In You alone, our true purpose is informed.
Almighty, Your all-seeing gaze, our every plight,
In Your boundless grace, we find our eternal light.

ELOHIM

Now I have fulfilled creation.
Man has now his mate in all perfection.
Man has now his mate in his own reflection.
They will grow together in one passion.

*(After some hours, Adam wakes up and finds a woman by him.
All royal angelic hosts and watchers are closely watching from
the realm of eternity).*

ADAM

Who are you in my resemblance?
Who are you in my vraisemblance?
Are you Lilith in re-incarnation?
Speak to me, I am lost in my imagination.

EVE

Who am I, and where am I here
Everything is strange, the wind I hear.
Which Garden is this with all its beauty?
Where everything around is so pretty?

*(As both Adam and Eve are looking at one another,
surprisingly, King Elohim from his throne thunders with a loud
voice as bright light flashes steadily on Adam's face like a
torch).*

ELOHIM

(Calling Adam)

Adam… Adam...
She is your kind, your helpmate
I created her for you, as a playmate
Your union is sanctified, be intimate
Love her always, teach her on how to relate.

(Uproar Continues).

ELOHIM

*(King Elohim lifting his two hands to the kingdom Earth and the
direction of Adam and eve begins to bless them).*

You are the crown of creation
You're the crown of all perfection.
Be fruitful, multiply, and have dominion.
Have dominion over kingdoms and nations.

All watchers shall serve you in fellowship
All creation must reverence me in worship.
Whatever thing you bind on Earth,
Here in heaven, it is bound as on Earth.

Whatever you allow on Earth
Here in heaven, it is allowed as on Earth.
I have made you a god and king forever…
Heed my word, the Torah to live forever.
Now, creation must show their obeisance!

*(Chorus continues with the cherubim, singing, flapping
their six wings, flying around, and all the throne).*

CHORUS
Holy, Holy, Holy, Is Our King,
Unto you shall we praise and sing.
Who Was, and is, and lives forever.
We shall worship you wherever and whenever.

*(Enter Gabriel, Michael, Uriel, Raphael all bow down to honor
Adam. Then all the Angels, Archangels, Thrones, Lords,
Principalities, Powers, Cherubim, and Seraphim, except for
Lucifer who refuses to bow to Adam.)*

(Chorus Continues, Twenty-Four Elders Singing).

ELDERS
Worthy are You, Oh Great King, enthroned on high,
To receive honor, glory, and power, we testify.
Above all, creation's chorus in harmony does bring,
You shaped all existence, and for Your praise, we sing.

None could ever shape Your will, supreme and divine,
In Your perfect plan, all creation does align.
Inscribed in the Torah, Your wisdom does instill,
With love, You fashioned us, and in You, we fulfill.
Almighty, Your all-seeing gaze, our souls refine.

[EXEUNT]

ACT 2: SCENE 4

[An Extraterrestrial Kingdom]

(V.O. by Metatron Continues)

All heavenly hosts were convoked
To the judgment room with hazy smoke.
Every host feared, and nobody dared spoke
For someone was trying to carry an uneasy yoke.

It was an unusual call to the trial room
Every host waited in anticipation of their doom.
Every host had a feeling of despair or gloom,
Whenever such proceedings begin it's doom.

Yet, none knew what was to be their prognosis,
No host was intelligent enough or had gnosis.
Of what Elohim in his infinite power could do
Even Lucifer stood in fright, and terror too.

God's ways of judgment are not ordinary
Every evidence God puts clean and clear.
Suddenly appeared a gigantic mirror or screen,
Its length was endless, it was crystal clean.

(Enter other Watchers, Angels, Archangels, Thrones,
Lords, Principalities, Powers, Cherubim, and Seraphim
all trembling).

(Chorus continues with the cherubim, singing, flapping
their six wings, flying around, and all the throne).

CHORUS

Holy, Holy, Holy, our voices we raise,
To our King, we offer reverent praise.
Who was, is, and lives forevermore,
In Your presence, our spirits adore.

We shall worship You, wherever we stand,
In every moment, at Your command.
With hearts full of love, our voices we bring,
To the eternal King, our praises we sing.

(Appears a Divine Throne, with big a book written on it
"THE TORAH").

(V.O. by Metatron Continues)

The Torah was written with black fire on white fire.
A big book, with burning flames like a campfire.
It was lying on the Divine Throne of King Elohim
Nobody ever sat on this throne, nobody, nothing —

Pages of the book began to open, it could speak
Every host lost hope, the omen before them was bleak
The Torah then stops flipping its pages
The book seemed to have survived for ages.

ELOHIM

(V.O. by Metatron Continues)

I am who I am.
I am what I am.
I Am the Ancient of Days.
I Am the Father of All Lights.

I Am the El-Shaddai-The Almighty King.
I Am the Elohim-The Omnipotent King.
I Am the El-Elyon- The Most High King.

I Am El-Olam.The Everlasting King.

I Am the El-Roi-The King Who Sees.
I Am the King of Hosts.
I am Elohim Chayim - The Living God.
I am El Elyon - The Most High God.

(Chorus continues with the cherubim, singing, flapping their six wings, flying around, and all the throne).

CHORUS

Holy, Holy, Holy, Is Our King,
Unto you shall we praise and sing.
Who Was, and is, and lives forever.
We shall worship you wherever and whenever.

ELOHIM

Now I want you to gaze with sight
I want you to see and gain insight.
I am the Almighty, with unlimited might.
On the second day of creation was hell
A place to torment all those who rebel.

(Suddenly appears a colossal cloud like spiritual portal leading to the underground kingdoms or hell. It is like an express highway, but on each side are all clouds of different colors and exits).

ELOHIM

There are seven heavens
There are seven Earths.

(Then the Seven Heavens and Earth appear in the portal)

Each separated by five tiers.
Layers of fire, perilous than it appears.

Erezis the seventh—
Above the lower Earth is a consecution of the Abyss.

The Tohu, Bohu, Sea and Waters—
Then the sixth Earth called Adamah.
Adam divided from the fifth Earth the Arka.
The abode of the Gehana, Sha'are Zalmawet,
Sha'are Mawet, Beer Shahat, Tit ha-Yawen
Abaddon, and Sheol.

(Angels Terrified)

Tebel, the second Earth
Home and abode for living creatures
Three hundred and sixty-five creatures
Different from any known-on Earth.

Other creatures are strange human beings
They have bodies of human beings,
But the head of a lion, ox, serpents.
Some of which are fierce in rage so argent

(Chorus Continues, Twenty-Four Elders Singing)

ELDERS

Worthy are You, Oh Great King
To receive honor, glory, and power...
You're, above all, all creatures before You sing.
You created all things, and by your power
For Your praise, every creation's duty is to sing.

No creature ever determined Your will
For all You made, created were in Your perfect will.
You've written Your will in the Torah with a fire quill
You created us in love, in You alone is our being.

You're the Almighty, Your eyes all-seeing.

ELOHIM

Next to the second Earth Tebel
Are two faced and head human creatures
Four hands, four feet as their natures.
Then the Earth of Adam, Helel —

I created 196, 000 worlds—a multiverse
This for my glory, and honor—

(Uproar and Murmuring).

ELOHIM

It takes five hundred years
To sojourn from Earth to heaven.
It takes five hundred years
To sojourn from East to West.

It takes five hundred years
To sojourn from North to South.
To sojourn from heaven's end to end.
My kingdom and power has not end.

*Chorus continues with the cherubim, singing, flapping
their six wings, flying around, and all the throne).*

CHORUS

Holy, Holy, Holy, Is Our King,
Unto you shall we praise and sing.
Who was, and is, and lives forever.
We shall worship you wherever and whenever.

ELOHIM

(Pointing to the East).

To the East is Paradise
A place and reward for the wise.
It has seven tiers or divisions
It is merited by wise free will decisions.

To the west, are great gigantic oceans
Upon it, there are islands and creatures in motions.

(Portals Appear)

Beyond the islands are infinite grasslands
Full of species of serpents with deadly glands
Scorpions with no mercy even to the plants.

To the North is hell-fire, snow, windstorm
Hailstones, ice, reserved for the stubborn.
It is also the abode of demons, evil spirits
A doomed place for the haughty in spirit.

To the south, is a storeroom reserved for fire
A dark cave of dense smoke to ever admire.
A storeroom where I forged all the hurricane
And can destroy within seconds and plain.

Both heaven and Earth to the west, east
South can meet with no friction or ease.
The north is for the trial of any insurrection
The trial chamber for any insubordination.

*(Chorus continues with the cherubim, singing, flapping
their six wings, flying around, and all the throne).*

CHORUS

Holy, Holy, Holy, our voices we raise,
To our King, we offer reverent praise.
Who was, is, and lives forevermore,

In Your presence, our spirits adore.

We shall worship You, wherever we stand,
In every moment, at Your command.
With hearts full of love, our voices we bring,
To the eternal King, our praises we sing.

(Piercing light from the Torah Flashing to the screen).

ELOHIM

Here comes the place of anguish
A place I wish none should perish.
You all have a free will, a treasure to cherish,
Choose wisely, don't be lured or be foolish.

Once cast into any of the division of hell
There is no hope, no other story to tell.
Hell has seven deadly sections of divisions
Each division is beneath the other divisions.

They're Shoel, Abaddon, Sha'are Mawet,
Tit ha-Yawen, Beer Shahat, Sha'are Zalmawet
And finally the Gehenna—
It takes three hundred years to traverse each.

Traverse its height, or traverse its width
Or traverse the depth or traverse each division
Each division in hell has seven subdivisions
In each sub-division are seven rivers of fire.

In each seven subdivisions are also hail fire.
Each division is guarded by Angels of Destruction
Nine thousand angels for each division,
For anyone who denies his creator's for destruction.

In every division are seven caves

In every cave, are seven thousand crevices;
In each crevice, are seven thousand scorpions,
Each scorpion has three hundred rings.
In each ring, are sacs of poisonous venoms…
Each venom has seven deadly rivers
This, no rebel can escape judgement
For my righteousness speaks even in judgement.

There is no mercy in hell—
It burns with five different fires.
A place never to ever think or aspire.
The first hell fire consumes and absorbs.

The second hell fire consumes and does absorb
The third hell fire absorbs but does not consume.
The fourth hell fire neither absorbs nor consumes
The fifth hell fire devours other fires…

Some hell fires are like hot or torrid coals;
Burning coals as huge as a mountain
Burning coals as huge as thousands of hills
Burning coals are large as the Dead Sea.

Burning coals as huge as rocks and stone
Burning coals rivers flowing with Sulphur,
The stones produce rivers of magma –
It's a full lake of burning sulphur.

*(Chorus continues with the cherubim, singing, flapping
their six wings, flying around, and all the throne).*

ELDERS

Worthy are You, Oh Great King
To receive honor, glory, and power...
You're, above all, all creatures before You sing.

You created all things, and by your power
For Your praise, every creation's duty is to sing.

No creature ever determined Your will
For all You made, created were in Your perfect will.
You've written Your will in the Torah with a fire quill
You created us in love, in You alone is our being.
You're the Almighty, Your eyes all-seeing.

ELOHIM

I AM the sovereign King, Immutable,
I created the Earth and water indispensable,
I created the air and fire unquenchable,
I created day and created night irrefutable.

I created the seen and unseen undisputable,
I created light and darkness both mutable
I created the unseen in nine classes indisputable,
I created them in three orders so compatible.

I AM the sovereign King, Immutable,
I created them all perfect and so indispensable,
Cherubim, Seraphim, and Thrones, all suitable.
Cherubim, wisdom of my creation and motion.

Seraphim wisdom of creation, fiery motion,
Thrones, wisdom of creation, fixed motion.
My throne bearers, glorious, so imputable,
I AM the sovereign King, Immutable.

I created them all perfect and so indispensable,
Lords, motion with might to conquer or subdue
Powers, motion to my will in full sight or view,
All I created for my pleasure and my view…

Rulers, motion rulers of the sun, moon, and stars,

Against the evil daring darts, aiming at the stars.
Lords, powers, and rulers, all formidable
I AM the sovereign King, Immutable.

I created them all perfect and so indispensable,
Principalities, motion, and rulers of all elements,
They rule with justice without any sentiment
My Kingdom is that of righteousness not sentiment.

Archangels, motion, and rulers of all creatures,
They rule and govern with invincible features.
Except one man, made or created in my nature,
Angels, the guardian of man, in his frail nature.

Principalities, archangels, and angels are all able,
All by my power, by my word so formidable.
All I have established will pass away in time
But my word, only my word surpasses time.

*(Chorus continues with the cherubim, singing, flapping
their six wings, flying around, and all the throne).*

CHORUS

Holy, Holy, Holy, Is Our King,
Unto you shall we praise and sing.
Who was, and is, and lives forever.
We shall worship you wherever and whenever.

[EXEUNT KING ELOHIM
and myriads of Angels dispersing]

ACT 2: SCENE 5

[An Extraterrestrial Kingdom]

(V.O. by Metatron Continues)

There are daring devil even in heaven
Pride motivate some to brave,
There will prefer to leave heaven for a cave.
They have seen their fate, the grave.

Lucifer still determined gathered some hosts
He acted as their boss and also host.
His heart was bitter, he was so enraged.
He feared no hell, he feared nobody' rage.

Pride blinded his eyes, and he desired honor
He was unhappy, prostrating to man was a dishonor.
A new camp will be formed in heaven
To challenge King Elohim's decision
And to thwart the plans of Elohim's vision.

(Lucifer and his Secret Insurrection Counsel).

(Enter Lucifer very furious, followed Beelzebub and other rebellious watchers).

LUCIFER

This is too much of a drama
King Elohim wants to cause a trauma.
Why create such a place for torment?
Is he planning to destroy us all in judgment?

REBEL

It did seem to use to us likewise
It all came to us as a surprise.

We need to be watchful and wise.
King Elohim is devising a vice.

LUCIFER

He destroyed ancient creations
This was before our creation.
We must not fall for his predation
We must put up a fight for liberation.

REBEL

We can't afford to lose our glory
We must preserve it even by means gory.
Could King Elohim be this insidious?
His judgment is very invidious.

LUCIFER

I am glad we see alike,
That you can see all this dislike.
How can we bow down to clay,
Something that will one day decay?

REBEL

(Laughing Sardonically).

He even created for Adam a Garden
A well-dressed garden called Eden.
Where else do you see such glamour?
We must form our army and forge our armor.

LUCIFER

(Pointing the Glamour Of Eden)

On the third day of creation
Elohim created for Adam a Paradise
He created two gates, with a deadly device
To secure its entrance from us creation.

REBEL

Aren't we not supposed to be his creation?
This gives us a very negative impression.
That others are more important to him.
Why must we continue to trust him?

LUCIFER

Sixty myriads angels keep him watch
To provide him security — top notch.
Each guardian angel is heavenly lustrous.
He only clothes his chosen at the gate
For those he hates, he calls them ingrate.

REBEL

(Looking at Eden's entrance Gate).

We must have a master plan
We must act before we're banned.
We have seen the omen so bleak
We must not act frail or even weak.

LUCIFER

We are intelligently gifted
Adam can't do anything if not assisted.
He can't succeed without our perspicacity
We shall bring him down by audacity or edacity

REBEL

How can clay be of any wit?
Did King Elohim think Adam to be fit
To rule a whole kingdom of luminaries?
We can't bow to these trivialities.

LUCIFER

I will seek audience with the King

I ask to challenge Adam in anything
The winner will bow and serve the other
If I win, Adam will be under our order.

REBEL

We can't wait to see Adam's humiliation,
The humiliation of an eternal annihilation.
Hell will be thrilled to see this damnation.
The North will be his next destination.

LUCIFER

King Elohim did well to create hell,
It might end up as Adam's eternal cell.
He will rot in there, tortured and swell,
I am glad it takes years to cross hell's ell.

REBEL

(Laughter and uproar).

We shall also contest to take Eden
The resplendent of all the gardens…
It won't hurt requesting four gates
To accommodate every creature or primates.

LUCIFER

I would want to have King Elohim
Be at the gate as a keeper or night watch.
He will be my messenger at will to dispatch.
He will know he has an equipotent match.

REBEL

What of Michael and Gabriel?
What of Uriel and Raphael?
They could be our very good buddies.
Let them act as our coned dummies.

LUCIFER

They are all Elohim's puppet.
They are only good as his trumpet.
In a single combat, I will crush them
Worry not, they are already condemned.

REBEL

(Uproar and chanting).

Lucifer! Lucifer! Lucifer!

[EXEUNT]

[Earth—Garden of Eden]

Elohim, in radiant glory, graces the scene,
Michael, Raphael, Uriel, and Gabriel, their presence
keen, Heavenly hosts, in harmonious chorus, their voices
ring, Cherubim, with six wings, their praises they sing,
Flapping, flying around, adorning the throne,
A celestial symphony, in Eden's garden, beautifully
shown.

CHORUS

Holy, Holy, Holy, Is Our King,
Unto you shall we praise and sing.
Who was, and is, and lives forever.
We shall worship you wherever and whenever.

(Suddenly a cloudy spiritual portal mirror with the colors of the
rainbow or aura appears before Adam. Adam can see Elohim
and the heavenly hosts all around Eden).

ADAM

Eve —
Haste, haste —
King Elohim is here
Let's bow for him in holy fear.

He's the Alpha and the Omega
The light of heaven lights our lineage
He has come for us to have fellowship
He has come with other companionship.

(Enter other creatures in Eden, male and female).

ELOHIM

Let all creation worship me in majesty
Let all creation sing for me in honesty.
All I created is perfect and good,
Leaves of tree for healing and food.
Crushed house flies to heal sores
Caused by hornet stings.

Animals were created to serve man,
Adam as you see is may master plan.
Creatures that prostate to him do it to me
He is my image, I am in him, he is in me.

*(Michael, Gabriel, Uriel, Raphael fall prostrate before Adam in
reverence, other celestial host follow, then the rest of the
creation in Eden).*

Man has me contained in the Torah,
Man has the Torah contained in his heart.
My will for creation is not too hard
For man on this Earth rules by my hand.

Animals have my Torah in their conscience
I'm the Almighty, Omnipotent, and Omniscience.
Even without the Torah given to man
Animals can teach man morality in plan.

Does the cat not cover its excrement?
Isn't it worth of morality or excitement?
Look at my holy creation the ant,
It minds its business and with jot it chants.

Each creation has their language of praise
All is to my glory; I understand every phrase.
The Earth, hell, paradise, trees all do reverence
Many others, I can cite for reference.
Does the cock not crow seven times

When I walk in Paradise all the times?

*(Chorus continues with the cherubim, singing, flapping
their six wings, flying around, and all the throne).*

CHORUS

Holy, Holy, Holy, our voices do ring,
To our King, unceasing praises we bring.
Who was, and is, and will live on forever,
In Your presence, our devotion will never sever.

Wherever and whenever, our worship shall be,
In every moment, we bend our hearts to Thee.
With love and reverence, our voices take wing,
To the eternal King, our praises shall cling.

*(All creation in the garden and heavenly hosts begin in loud
voice to worship, each using their language or method of praise
or worship).*

Adam, I have given you Paradise
I am here to teach you for you to be wise.
I created two gates entry to paradise
Sixty myriads of angels for your security.

The glory of each myriad is glorious in dignity.
This is what will happen to your descendants
They will enter Paradise based on their ascendant.
If they keep the Torah, when they come to the gate.

After they have died, I'll show mercy and not berate.
They shall be arrayed with seven glorious garments
And will receive two crowns of merriment.
Eight myrtles in the hands for a life merited.

They shall dwell in Paradise and be respected.

Eighty myriads of trees stand at every corner of paradise,
Every corner has sixty myriads of angels signing
In the middle is a tree of life with fruits swinging.

These fruits have fifteen thousand tastes
Each taste is different from each in a unique taste.
Paradise has seven of its kinds or divisions,
Twelve myriads of miles from each other….

(Chorus continues, Twenty-Four elders singing).

ELDERS

Worthy are You, Oh Great King
To receive honor, glory, and power...
You're, above all, all creatures before You sing.
You created all things, and by your power
For Your praise, every creation's duty is to sing.

No creature ever determined Your will
For all You made, created were in Your perfect will.
You've written Your will in the Torah with a fire quill
You created us in love, in You alone is our being.
You're the Almighty, Your eyes all-seeing.

ELOHIM

(To Adam)

Adam! Adam! Adam!
You are the pious seed for the next generation.
You have the Torah, for generation's veneration.
I have made you out of my image for the Kingdom.

A tree stands in the middle of Eden,
Whose fruits, must not be eaten.
All other fruits, herbs, roots can be eaten.
The day you eat, you' all be smitten.

ELOHIM
(To Eve)

Paradise is vast too complex,
You have the intellect that is much more complex.
Adam will assigned to north and east
He shall name all males animals
You will be assigned to the south and west
You shall name all female animals.

(Adam and Eve prostrating before king Elohim).

*(Chorus continues with the cherubim, singing, flapping
their six wings, flying around, and all the throne).*

CHORUS
Holy, Holy, Holy, Is Our King,
Unto you shall we praise and sing.
Who was, and is, and lives forever.
We shall worship you wherever and whenever.

(All creation also join in chorus).

[EXEUNT KING ELOHIM
Heavenly Host Back To Heaven]

[An Extraterrestrial Kingdom]

(Lucifer, who has left his praise office for a while now, comes before Elohim to request an intellectual challenge with Adam).

(Enter other celestial Hosts Angels, Archangels, Thrones, Lords, Principalities, Powers, Cherubim, and Seraphim, all trembling).

(Chorus continues with the cherubim, singing, flapping their six wings, flying around, and all the throne).

CHORUS

Holy, Holy, Holy, Is Our King,
Unto you shall we praise and sing.
Who was, and is, and lives forever.
We shall worship you wherever and whenever.

(Appears a Divine Throne, with big a book written on it THE TORAH).

ELOHIM

I am the only King all powerful -
I needed courtiers on whom to be merciful.
I needed an army so strong and powerful
So, I created you all so wonderful.

(Yelling With Joy).

Long time ago in my omniscience,
I conceived to create man; I sought an alliance,
But some luminaries were of non-compliance.
They failed me and were seriously in defiance.

(Astonishment is seen in all innocent faces except that of Lucifer and his team)

ELOHIM

(Continues).

Not all hosts were in one opinion
To create man and grant him all dominion.
They were jealous not to have other creatures
Especially man who is to take my nature.

Some cried, "What is man, that you are so mindful…
He's lower than us in glory but very meaningful."
Some cried, "What is the son of man to always visit,
You have made him lower, but with a strong spirit."

(Rebellious watchers murmuring).

ELOHIM

There was opposition so in vexation,
I consumed them all in my indignation.
Only Michael survived, with few others
Those who were all loyal to my will and orders.

I took an oath by the Torah to avoid destruction.
I promised justice in place of annihilation.
I am bound by my Word, the Torah in all situations.
Not to act against my sovereign will written.
Anyone acting against it will be destroyed or smitten.

(Chorus Continues, Twenty-Four Elders Singing)

ELDERS

Worthy are You, Oh Great King

To receive honor, glory, and power...
You're, above all, all creatures before You sing.
You created all things, and by your power
For Your praise, every creation's duty is to sing.

No creature ever determined Your will
For all You made, created were in Your perfect will.
You've written Your will in the Torah with a fire quill
You created us in love, in You alone is our being.
You're the Almighty, Your eyes all-seeing.

ELOHIM

I am infallible, but man is fallible.
Despite his fallibility, he is valuable.
For this purpose, you were all created.
Beware, not to become conceited.

(Enter Lucifer to provoke King Elohim to anger).

LUCIFER

Great King—
If Adam is of clay, frail and fallible
How can he compare with us infallible?
His fallibility makes him less honorable.
What is man, a creature much dishonorable?

ELOHIM

My will is final for all creation.
I refrain my wrath from any annihilation.
I am the Torah, and I am bound by it
Only my will in it shall be done indeed.

LUCIFER

I am glad you are bound by it
So that we can think over your deed.
Destructive force is not always a solution,

I am glad you have taken a wise resolution.

MICHAEL
(Pulling out his sword ready to strike as every other creature is shocked with the manner in which he addresses Elohim).

ELOHIM
Peace Michael, be still at peace and at ease.
The wages for transgression is death
Beware, I will punish it to its depth.
My wrath knows no mercy in punishing
Any willful transgressor—

LUCIFER
(Mockingly).

Michael is just as frail as Adam's clay.
Hold yourself, and stand not on my way.
In a single combat, you'll be like crumbs
To be easily crushed with my two thumbs…

Like a crumb of bread to the mercy of an ant
So are you to my thumb, so irrelevant.
You're just a petty jester who gallivants
No need to waste time with a licker irrelevant.

(Agitations).

ELOHIM
Enough Lucifer!
Your heart has been engulfed by darkness.
I am still ready to restore your happiness,
If you are willing to show penitence
For this sacrilegious offence.

LUCIFER

I am neither a criminal for penitence
Nor do I need or require repentance.
Should defending my opinion be a transgression?
Michael needs penitence for his aggression?

ELOHIM

I don't desire any war in my kingdom
I mapped the world in great wisdom.
I created everything in its place
Not with intention to have any erased.

LUCIFER

Only cowards dread to war
They play to be noble, even against the wall.
We can still end this in a peaceful accord
Which the Torah will officially keep a record…

ELOHIM

What is your peaceful accord
Which you want to go into a record?
Has clay become wiser than its potter?
We are open to your suggestion or order.

LUCIFER

Oh King! I love your great humility
You could be a great leader with ability
If only you consulted my opinion or sanity,
Before taking any decision in tranquility.

ELOHIM

You are so daring Lucifer…
Lucky are you that I made a vow
That I will never destroy creation again
But remember, I am the law.

Speak your resolution

If that suffices your absolution.
The heavens and Earth are willing to hear
Speak, don't be diplomatic, get rid of fear.

LUCIFER

I will challenge Adam's erudition
If he passes the requested conditions,
I will bow down to him in any situation.
If he fails, he will bow to me in humiliation.

ELOHIM

You are very brave, Lucifer!
Have you thought of what you will suffer,
If you fail to meet up with Adam's wit?
Do you think you can win in this bit?

LUCIFER

My King… Why not save some energy
Or even gather all your synergy
To get Adam ready for this tragic day?
A day I call his doom's day or D-day.

ELOHIM

Adam does not require preparation.
He has been ready from the foundation
When I mapped out the world in creation.
That D-day, creation will see your humiliation.

LUCIFER

We shall meet in the Garden
I shall be the new owner of Eden
I will see you all before tomorrow's dusk
Adam will be reduced back to dust—

(Chorus Continues, Twenty-Four elders singing).

ELDERS

Worthy are You, Oh Great King
To receive honor, glory, and power...
You're, above all, all creatures before You sing.
You created all things and by your power
For Your praise, every creation's duty is to sing.

No creature ever determined Your will
For all You made, created were in Your perfect will.
You've written Your will in the Torah with a fire quill
You created us in love, in You alone is our being.
You're the Almighty, Your eyes all-seeing.

[EXIT LUCIFER]

ACT 3: SCENE 2

[Earth— Garden of Eden]

(Enter Elohim, Michael, Raphael, Uriel, Gabriel, and other loyal heavenly hosts to visit Adam in the garden of Eden).

(Chorus continues with the cherubim, singing, flapping their six wings, flying around, and all the throne).

CHORUS

Holy, Holy, Holy, Is Our King,
Unto you shall we praise and sing.
Who was, and is, and lives forever.
We shall worship you wherever and whenever.

(Suddenly a cloudy spiritual portal mirror with the colors of the rainbow or aura appears before Adam. Adam can see Elohim and the heavenly hosts all around Eden)

ADAM

Eve —
Haste, haste —
King Elohim is here
Elohim is here with the watchers…
Let's bow for him in holy fear

Open our hearts to his message hear,
He's the Alpha and the Omega
He has come for us to have fellowship
He has come with other companionship.

ELOHIM

Peace unto your soul!
Peace, be you consoled.

Your soul is more precious than gold.
Your soul is very ancient and old.

ADAM

What is a soul?
Part of my feet called sole?
Is that another animal or creation?
And where is this soul's location?

ELOHIM

Your soul was created on the first day
Your soul is eternal and does not decay.
Your body will return to its originator
The Earth as willed by me the creator.

ADAM

Does it mean I am the first in creation?
Though my body was last in formation?
Why not create my soul and body together?
Aren't they from the same source and father?

ELOHIM

You pre-existed before all creation
You are the seal of all divine perfection.
My Spirit hovered over the rivers and waters
To make sure your soul was not altered.

ADAM

If my soul pre-existed before creation
Who could alter my soul in alteration?
Were there any other souls in pre-creation
Who could oppose my formation?

ELOHIM

I created them all, all souls are mine.
I have created the souls of all generations

I have given them all specific designs.
Each soul has powers given at creation.

ADAM

Power in every soul at creation?
If all souls are created for all generations
Where are they kept; I mean their locations?
I need more of these mysteries or revelations.

ELOHIM

Within every soul is the divine power,
The power to ascend and go higher.
All souls are before my throne as a choir
They sing praises to me every given hour.

From your soul they were all created
Making you their father most celebrated.
Everything created on this Earth and world
Was planned to bow to you, even my staff.

ADAM

So, my soul has been cloned?
How in the human body are they enthroned?
When are their physical bodies composed?

ELOHIM

I match every soul to a sperm
I give it a human body in the womb.
Where they grow and reach their full term.
As woman's womb is, so in heaven is a room
Where souls still to be born await their Earthly costume.

ADAM

Do you then control their fate?
Who determines others to be born great,
While others are born poor, others rich?

Do you control their free will for each?

ELOHIM

I designed each soul for good deeds.
I determine if they are male or female
I didn't create any soul for evil or to wail.
Every soul has a free will to succeed or fail.

ADAM

Do angels have a free will to decide?
Do angels have a free will to backslide?
Can angels sin, or refuse to obey instructions?
Can angels carry on an act of reproduction?

ELOHIM

All creation or hosts are fallible.
They can fall or even become unstable
Of free will if a test of true love from creation.
Perfect love cast out fear for damnation.

(Enter Lucifer in Eden).
*(Michael, Uriel, Gabriel, Raphael, sounding a trumpet,
gathering all creation in the garden).*

LUCIFER

Did you prepare his mind already?
I hope his frail mind is not unsteady?
I won't spare him in this mortal combat.
Poor Adam… a little brat!

(Chorus Continues, Twenty-Four Elders Singing)

ELDERS

Worthy are You, Oh Great King
To receive honor, glory, and power...

You're, above all, all creatures before You sing.
You created all things and by your power
For Your praise, every creation's duty is to sing.

No creature ever determined Your will
For all You made, created were in Your perfect will.
You've written Your will in the Torah with a fire quill
You created us in love, in You alone is our being.
You're the Almighty, Your eyes all-seeing.

(Exit Lucifer)

ELOHIM

Adam is the perfect seal of all wisdom
His wisdom is unique in my kingdom
I know your wisdom's limit or foolishness,
Today all creation will see your callousness.

(Creation Cheering)

Adam! Adam! Adam!

ELOHIM
(To Lucifer).

Lucifer—
What's the name of this beast?

(Pointing to a cow).

LUCIFER

Such a beast I have never seen
Did you just create him on this scene?
I don't think it has a name either.
Let Adam fumble, he won't either.

ELOHIM

(To Adam)

Adam—
What the name of this…

ADAM

My King,
This is beast is called a COW!

ELOHIM

Correct!

(Creation yelling in happiness)

ELOHIM
(To Lucifer now).

Lucifer—
This is your second chance
You must prove your wit and stance.
What is the name of this other beast?

(Pointing to an Ox).

LUCIFER
(Fumbling to find an answer, but nothing comes)

ELOHIM

Let me help you,
The name begins with letter O…

(Lucifer fumbles again big time)

LUCIFER

Oath… em… oozing….

ELOHIM

(To Lucifer)

You failed again….

ELOHIM
(To Adam)

Adam—
What the name of this—

ADAM

My King,
This is beast is called an OX!

LUCIFER

(Lucifer so disappointed screams so loud that his voice is heard in heaven).

(Michael, Uriel, Gabriel, Raphael, and other heavenly hosts prostrating before Adam, with Michael taking lead, except lucifer and a few of his rebels. other creatures in Eden prostate before him).

ELOHIM

Lucifer—
Do you admit Adam's superiority,
That is your master, your seniority?
You have lost before all eyes in the garden
They have seen you guilt-smitten.

LUCIFER

Clay is never superior to fire!
There is nothing in him that I admire.
He looks like one created from a mire
Who is and will soon expire—

(Exit Lucifer angrily to heaven).

(Chorus continues with the cherubim, singing, flapping their six wings, and flying around the throne).

CHORUS
Holy, Holy, Holy, Is Our King,
Unto you shall we praise and sing.
Who was, and is, and lives forever.
We shall worship you wherever and whenever.

[EXEUNT]

**[Empyrean Heaven —
Extraterrestrial Kingdom]**

*(Enter Michael, Gabriel, Raphael, and Uriel
within the empyrean heaven before the war in heaven).*

*(Chorus by the cherubim, singing, flapping their six
wings, flying around, and all the throne).*

CHORUS

Holy, Holy, Holy, our voices proclaim,
To our King, we lift a reverent acclaim.
Who was, and is, and will remain ever,
In Your presence, our devotion we endeavor.

Wherever, whenever, our worship ascends,
In each moment, our faith steadfastly extends.
With love and reverence, our praises take flight,
To the eternal King, our hearts' pure delight.

*(Michael, Gabriel, Raphael, and Uriel prostrating before the
throne of Elohim in reverence).*

(Chorus Continues, Twenty-Four Elders Singing).

ELDERS

Worthy, Oh Great King, beyond compare,
To receive honor, glory, and power, we declare.
Above all, creation's chorus does take wing,
You, Creator of all, hear the songs they bring.

Each creature's duty, to sing in Your praise,
By Your mighty hand, all life You raise.
In Your perfect will, all things do fulfill,

Inscribed in the Torah, with a fire quill.

In love, You formed us, our essence, our core,
In You alone, our true being we explore.
Almighty, Your all-seeing gaze, ever keen,
Guides us through life's paths, the unseen.

(Enter Elohim On Chariot Of Fire).

ELOHIM

I am what I am.
I Am the Ancient of Days.
I Am the Father of All Lights.

I Am the El-Shaddai-The Almighty King.
I Am the Elohim-The Omnipotent King.
I Am the El-Elyon- The Most High King.
I Am El-Olam.The Everlasting King.

I Am the El-Roi-The King Who Sees.
I Am the King of Hosts.
I am Elohim Chayim - The Living God.
I am El Elyon - The Most High God.

(Chorus Continues, Twenty-Four Elders Singing).

ELDERS

Worthy are You, Oh Great King
To receive honor, glory, and power...
You're, above all, all creatures before You sing.
You created all things and by your power
For Your praise, every creation's duty is to sing.

No creature ever determined Your will
For all You made, created were in Your perfect will.
You've written Your will in the Torah with a fire quill

You created us in love, in You alone is our being.
You're the Almighty, Your eyes all-seeing.

(Repeating king Elohim's attributes with a louder male voice like an army ready for war).

You are the El-Shaddai
You are the Elohim
You are the El-Elyon
You are the El-Roi
You are the El-Olam.
You are the Lord of Hosts.

ELOHIM

My kingdom is at war!
An outrageous war never fought before.
One of the princes is gathering a battalion
He has enticed many watchers in his rebellion.

MICHAEL

Oh, Great King—
Who is this prince of rebellion?
Lucifer, who has been like a hellion?
He has always given such an impression
Lately, he has been acting with aggression.

ELOHIM

He wants to devastate my Kingdom
He deceived many with his corrupt wisdom.
Many shall fall from their habitation.
Many have pledged to him their cooperation.

GABRIEL

Oh, Great King— We can stop him…
We can persuade him; we can stop them.
Oh, Great King, let's allow this war.

Oh, Great King, many might fall.

ELOHIM

His heart is full of darkness and vice.
He won't listen or take to any advice.
He thinks to be so strong and wise
He wants to see with his own eyes.

MICHAEL

He does not seem to see his match
All watchers must keep their watch.
No persuasion might stop his determination.
I am not still sure of his true motivation.

ELOHIM

His termination is very ferocious
His motivations are dark and atrocious.
Michael, you are his elder in creation
He fears you, but beware of his confrontation

GABRIEL

Can't Michael alone take him down?
Compared to Michael, he is still a clown.
He might not have a strong army or battalion.
Our prince of war can suppress any rebellion.

ELOHIM

Beelzebub created as a trusted seraph
Joined Lucifer's rebellion with great wrath.
He will be the second commander-in-chief.
Lucifer will be the commander-in-chief.

GABRIEL

Beelzebub!
Second in command?
Now I begin to fully understand!

Our army is superior to withstand.

ELOHIM

Lucifer, at all costs, wants my throne
All resistance his way will be overthrown.
He will overthrow the empyrean guards
Be of good courage, the war will be hard.

MICHAEL

Oh, Great King!
Will Lucifer and Beelzebub succeed?
My army is big to suppress their conceit.
He can't have access to the empyrean.
We won't let him access the empyrean.

ELOHIM

Lucifer and his army
Shall kill millions of ophanim
He shall kill millions of seraphim
He shall kill millions of cherubim.

But don't worry, I am the creator of light -
Their dead bodies will rise or resurrect
To form an empyrean guard— Merkabah
Lucifer's army will be completely wrecked.

MICHAEL

(Yelling in a victorious battle cry).

ELOHIM

*(From the empyrean heaven, a beam of sharp light
points to a standing army ready for battle)*

Michael—
The army you commanded is corrupt
Swindled but this army is ready with might

These are the remnants ready to fight.
I am the Lord of Hosts.

800,000 Angels with daggers of fire,
700,000 Horsemen in chariots of fire,
600,000 Shield bearers
500,000 Bearers of axes of fire,
1,000,000 Slingers.
700,000 Torch bearers
300,000 Bearers of fiery crosses
400,000 Bearers of lamps.
120,000 Horsemen.

(Chorus continues with the Cherubim, singing, flapping their six wings, flying around, and all the throne).

CHORUS

Holy, Holy, Holy, Is Our King,
Unto you shall we praise and sing.
Who was, and is, and lives forever.
We shall worship you wherever and whenever.

(Chorus Continues Twenty-Four Elders Singing)

ELDERS

Worthy, Oh Great King, we humbly proclaim,
To receive honor, glory, and power, Your name.
Above all, creatures harmoniously sing,
You, Creator of all, to You, praises cling.

Every creation's purpose, a song to bring,
By Your power, for Your praise, they take wing.
No creature dictates Your divine skill,
All created in Your perfect, sovereign will.

Inscribed in the Torah, like a sacred quill's art,

Your will is written, a guiding, sacred chart.
In love, You formed us, our essence decreeing,
In You alone, our being finds its true meaning.

[EXEUNT]

[Extraterrestrial Kingdom – Heaven]

(Pre-war rally by Lucifer and his army)

(Enter Lucifer, Beelzebub, Samael, Belial, Balrog, and rebel watchers).

REBEL

(Chanting).

> Lucifer! Lucifer! Lucifer!
> Truly you alone can see far!
> You are the bright and morning star.
> You are our leader; you are our superstar.

LUCIFER

I am the older of all creation.
I witnessed other watchers' formation.
I know their power and their weakness.
Their weakness should not be seen as meekness.

REBEL

(Clapping).

> We can't trust Elohim anymore
> He can't continue to lead us anymore.
> His deeds are secretive and hideous.
> We much be watchful; he is very insidious!

REBEL

(Chanting).

> Lucifer! Lucifer! Lucifer!

Truly you alone can see far!
You are the bright and morning star.
You are our leader; you are our superstar.

LUCIFER

Elohim has a plan of execution
Opposing him is the only solution.
He plans execute us all in favor of Adam.
That is why without consent he created Adam.

REBEL

(Clapping).

LUCIFER

We must fight this fight together
Or we will all perish altogether.
We can't trust him, even Michael
We can't trust him, even Gabriel.

REBEL

Michael will be our main resistance.
We will need a stronger assistance.
He seems to have all the great military
With great skills that are exemplary.

LUCIFER

Be still! Be still and courageous
Our determination alone is rampageous.
Michael is of my rank, but I am superior.
He looks strong but is an inferior warrior.

REBEL

(Chanting)

Lucifer! Lucifer! Lucifer!
Truly you alone can see far!

You are the bright and morning star.
You are our leader; you are our superstar.

Freedom Now! Freedom Now!

LUCIFER

We are more than champions
We have millions of battalions
Who will be fighting for their freedom,
After which they will over this kingdom.

REBEL

(Clapping).

LUCIFER

I will be your commander in chief
I will fight against mischief.
I will fight for your freedom.
We shall dwell in a peaceful kingdom.

REBEL

(Chanting).

Lucifer! Lucifer! Lucifer!
Truly you alone can see far!
You are the bright and morning star.
You are our leader; you are our superstar.

LUCIFER

Beelzebub is the second commander in chief,
A seraph of honor who wants a shift.
An arch commander, sturdy and very swift,
Together, we will invade the empyrean heaven.

BEELZEBUB

REBEL

(Clapping).

LUCIFER

Belial—
An anointed cherubim of devouring fire,
He is to Elohim with every desire.
He will be my First Lieutenant
His wrath has no limit nor inclement.

BELIAL

(Legions of corrupt watchers align behind him).

LUCIFER

Gothmog, prince of Balrog -
My fearless first-line Lieutenants
He can break anything with his massive axe
Michael's army will melt like wax.

GOTHMOG

(Balrogs align behind Gothmog).

REBEL

(Clapping).

LUCIFER

Throne Warriors
  Orobas: Commander of 20 legions
  Pruflas: Commander of 26 legions
  Purson: Commander of 22 legions
  Forneus: Commander of 29 legions
  Phenix: Commander of 20 legions
  Murmur: Commander of 30 legions
  Focalor: Commander of 30 legions

(Enter all throne warrior commanders, followed by their legions lined up behind them).

LUCIFER

Power Warriors
>**Bael:** Commander of 66 legions
>Bael a three-headed creature.
>Each head represents a different animal
>a Human, a Toad, and a Cat.
>
>**Beleth:** Commander of 85 legions
>**Amy:** Commander of 36 legions
>**Crocell:** Commander of 48 legions
>**Vual:** Commander of 37 legions.
>**Gaap:** Commander of 25 legions

(Enter all power warrior commanders, followed by their legions lined up behind them).

LUCIFER

Dominion Powers
>**Marchosias**: Commander of 39 legions
>**Balam:** Commander of 40 legions

(Enter all dominion powers commanders, followed by their legions lined up behind them).

LUCIFER

Our warfare is very strategic
We must put Elohim's army into panic.
We have the best warriors and commanders
Michael's army is as weak as many salamanders.

REBEL

(Chanting)

LUCIFER

(To Beelzebub).

While the war is fierce and ongoing
We shall sneak without anyone knowing.
We shall attack the empyrean guards
We shall invade Elohim's throne with disregard.

BEELZEBUB

Lucifer, my lord,
We are ready to destroy and bombard.
We shall win the empyrean combat.
We shall trample Elohim's army as a doormat.
Michael will be our slave and bastard.

REBEL

(Chanting).

Lucifer! Lucifer! Lucifer!
With your vision, distances blur,
The morning star, shining afar,
Our leader, like a radiant star.

In your brilliance, we find our way,
Guiding us through night and day,
Our superstar, shining so bright,
Leading us with celestial light.

[EXEUNT]

[An Extraterrestrial Kingdom]

(Enter Elohim, Michael, Raphael, Uriel, Gabriel, and other loyal heavenly hosts).

(Chorus continues with the cherubim, singing, flapping their six wings, flying around, and all the throne).

CHORUS

Holy, Holy, Holy, our King divine,
In praise and song, to you, we incline.
Eternal, unchanging, you endure,
In worship, our hearts forever secure.

With reverence, we lift our voice,
In your presence, we rejoice.
You, the One who reigns supreme,
In your love, our souls redeem.

ELOHIM

My mercy has not still expired
Despite all what has transpired.
If you are here today, I assume
That you are back to yourself I presume.

LUCIFER

My King,
By assumption, you might be wrong
My willpower is still very strong.
I am here today, before this throng
Not for us to have this battle prolonged.

ELOHIM

My patience will run out of time

I gave you time to make up your mind.
Do not set a bad example for others'
Don't poison their minds to defile my orders.

LUCIFER

My King,
I am not the only one unhappy
Clay is an ugly substance very scrappy.
Why should luminaries be this humiliated?
They have long waited to be liberated.

ELOHIM

Are you now the voice of liberation
That is leading a vicious insurrection?
Beware that the abyss's is never full
Anyone that follows you is a fool.

LUCIFER

There must be a leader everywhere
To stand and decry what is unfair.
We are many of us asking for our rights -
What is right is, clay cannot be the light.

ELOHIM

I am the ultimate ruler, no coregent
I am the King Elohim the Omnipotent
You are not my equal or equipotent.
The Torah is my only retrain at the moment.

LUCIFER

My King,
We know the Torah is highly exalted
Above your throne highly escorted.
Truth at the same time can't be halted.
You are infallible, but can also be faulted.

ELOHM

Restrain your tongue from what is hellish
I delight not for any of you to perish.
If your free will lead you against the sword
Then, be ready for its ultimate reward.

LUCIFER

My King,
One more test or request
I will wrestle Michael in a contest.
If Michael wins, let judgment prevail
And let mercy not be of any travail.

ELOHIM

If that be your requested fate,
I will grant it to you without debate.
Gather your army, let them be in regiments
Michael, shall strike back with no sentiments.

LUCIFER

My King—
My army has long waited long for this.
We shall fight and win with ease.
We are certain we fight for justice
And for justice we shall fight for peace.

ELOHIM

Lucifer, Brace yourself and military
No time to waste, not dilatory.
Michael, for this hour I prepared you
Gather your valiant angels of war

(Lucifer and his supporters match to one side of heaven).

I am what I am.
I Am the Ancient of Days.

I Am the Father of All Lights.

I Am the El-Shaddai-The Almighty King.
I Am the Elohim-The Omnipotent King.
I Am the El-Elyon- The Most High King.
I Am El-Olam.The Everlasting King.

I Am the El-Roi-The King Who Sees.
I Am the King of Hosts.
I am Elohim Chayim - The Living God.
I am El Elyon - The Most High God.

(Chorus continues with the cherubim, singing, flapping their six wings, flying around, and all the throne).

CHORUS
Holy, Holy, Holy, our Sovereign King,
To you our praises and songs we bring.
You were, you are, and will be evermore,
In worship, our hearts to you we implore.

In every place and at every hour,
With reverence, we feel your power.
You, the Eternal One, we adore,
Our devotion to you forevermore.

LUCIFER
(To his army).

Real lions do not roar
They keep calm, sleep, and snore.
Today brings your redemption, be all brave.
Michael and his host will be our slaves...

(Yelling from Lucifer's army).

ELOHIM

(To Michael).

> You are my battle axe for punishment.
> You will restore peace in my government
> Darkness shall be banished indefinitely.
> Peace and tranquility will reign definitely.

(Chorus Continues, Twenty-Four Elders Singing)

ELDERS

Worthy are You, Oh Great King
To receive honor, glory, and power...
You're, above all, all creatures before You sing.
You created all things, and by your power
For Your praise, every creation's duty is to sing.

No creature ever determined Your will
For all You made, created were in Your perfect will.
You've written Your will in the Torah with a fire quill
You created us in love, in You alone is our being.
You're the Almighty, Your eyes all-seeing.

[EXEUNT]

ACT 3: SCENE 6

[An Extraterrestrial Kingdom]

(V.O. by Metatron Continues)

Finally, war broke up in heaven
With two opposing camps of armies in heaven.
Huge armies was formed by angelic creatures
They were creatures with terrifying features.

They were arranged in groups of seven
Every squad answerable to its commander.
Michael led King Elohim's camp or military
Lucifer led the rebellious angel's military.

The heavens were still for a while
With Elohim seated on the throne.
Lucifer yelled a battle cry so wild,
The atmosphere was tensed and hostile.

Suddenly, appeared creatures never seen
For Lucifer had been playing on Elohim's mercy.
They were armies to fight with Michael,
They looked like killing merciless machines.

Their sight alone changed the fighting scene
But Michael was confident with Elohim on the throne
The army of Lucifer was dissolved like wax
None of his armies could lift their ax.

It was too late to retreat from the battle
Michael crushed Lucifer's army like a beetle
It took Michael no effort to prove his might
Before an army that melted at his sight

(Enter Michael, Metatron, Raphael, Uriel, Gabriel, And Army).

MICHAEL

(Battle Cry)

Who is our King?

ARMY

(Chanting Military)

Elohim! Elohim! Elohim!

(Michael's military matching forward and lining up).

MICHAEL

(Battle Cry)

Who is our King?

ARMY

(Chanting Military)

Elohim! Elohim! Elohim!

MICHAEL

(To His Army)

Be on your guard!
Be on your guard!
With Elohim seated on the throne
Today, damnation will be served them.

Army

(Aligning following Michael's order)

(Chanting Songs Of Victory).

800,000 Angels with daggers of fire,
700,000 Horsemen in chariots of fire,
600,000 Shield bearers
500,000 Bearers of axes of fire,
1,000,000 Slingers,
700,000 Torch bearers
300,000 Bearers of fiery crosses
400,000 Bearers of lamps.
120,000 Horsemen.

MICHAEL

(Leading a battle cry).

In the grace of Elohim, the Almighty's hand,
We stand united, a courageous band.
With strength and purpose, we'll never lack,
As one, we rise and boldly attack!

Attack! Attack! Attack!
Attack! Attack! Attack!

LUCIFER

(To his army).

Strike once, with all our might,
Slay twice, in the darkest night.
Victory is ours, our hearts resound,
No retreat, no surrender, on hallowed ground!

BEELZEBUB

(Leading part of the army).

BELIAL

(Aligning his army)

GOTHMOG

(Aligning his army the Balrogs)

LUCIFER

(Inspecting the entire military).

Orobas: Matching into the battle with 20 legions
Pruflas: Matching into the battle with 26 legions
Purson: Matching into the battle with 22 legions
Forneus: Matching into the battle with 29 legions

Phenex: Matching into the battle with 20 legions
Murmur: Matching into the battle with 30 legions
Focalor: Matching into the battle with 30 legions
Bael: Matching into the battle with 66 legions

Beleth: Matching into the battle with 85 legions
Amy: Matching into the battle with 36 legions
Crocell: Matching into the battle with 48 legions
Vual: Matching into the battle with 37 legions.

Gaap: Matching into the battle with 25 legions
Marchosias: Matching into the battle with 39 legions
Balam: Matching into the battle with 40 legions

(Two militaries clashing, Michael and his troops defeated during the first, second, and third rounds of battle).

MICHAEL

(To his military)

Retreat!
    Retreat!
        Retreat!

(They are retreating he goes down on his knees and raises his hands in prayer).

Arise! Arise! Jehovah Sabaoth,
Let your enemies be scattered
Lord of lords, Lord of hosts!
Let your enemies be overpowered.

LUCIFER

(To his army, chanting)

Victory! Victory! Victory!
Press on, keep attacking with tenacity!
With hearts aflame, we'll never tire,
Onward we march, our spirits higher and higher!

(Michael and his military retreating with many casualties).

LUCIFER

(To some of his army)

Quick! Quick! Let's hasten our stride,
To the empyrean throne room, where destinies bide.
Elohim, prepare to face your impending gloom,
For my wrath shall consume, sealing your doom.

In the celestial chamber, we'll make our stand,
With courage and fury, we'll conquer the land.
Elohim's reign shall crumble and swoon,
As we rise to claim our empyrean boon.

(Lucifer leads an army to attack the empyrean guards)

EMPYREAN GUARDS

(Yelling for help)

Help! Help!
Michael, hear our plea!
The throne room is besieged, can't you see?

We're powerless to resist, unable to fight back,
In this great battle, we feel the impact, the attack.

The forces clash in this celestial fray,
In the empyrean's midst, where angels lay.
We look to you, Archangel of might,
To defend our realm and restore the light.

MICHAEL

(To Gabriel)

Retreat to the throne room.
The battle is very fierce, I assume.
Haste, the empyrean guards are pressured.
Haste, the empyrean room is our treasure.

GABRIEL

(Gabriel retreats to resist Lucifer from invading the throne room).

LUCIFER

(To his army).

We are taking over the throne
Elohim will soon be overthrown.
Elohim will soon be dethroned,
The throne is heaven's backbone.

GABRIEL

(To Lucifer).

We have to stop this senseless war
Why are killing one another for?
We are brothers, we must stop this war
We have lost lives in this uproar.

LUCIFER

Indeed we are brothers as you say.
All I ask from you is to have my way.
You are not my foe; Elohim is my target.
If you love as a brother, let's hit my target.

GABRIEL

(Resisting Lucifer from advancing).

Elohim is our king, so merciful
Drop your weapon and be remorseful.
He will forgive you, please, brother.
We must stop this war chaos and disorder.

LUCIFER

(Mounting Pressure).

I destroy everything on my way
I must get the throne without delay.
I will use more force if you insist.
No one dares me or even will resist.

(Enter Beelzebub to aid Lucifer).

GABRIEL

(Calling Michael for backup).

LUCIFER

(To Michael).
    You are a weak commander
    As weak as a salamander.
    I will crush your entirety to my heel
    They will become like dust in a field.

MICHAEL

You are a villain, you are a traitor

You have betrayed your creator.
You will pay for this rebellion.
For invading heaven's sacred pavilion.

(War against the empyrean room is intense, Beelzebub inflicting a lot of casualties).

MICHAEL
(He overpowers Lucifer as he falls helpless on the battlefront. Michael puts his dagger, ready to decapitate him).

Call your army to order
Call them to order and surrender!
Enough of this killing you murderer.
This is your last chance; you won't have another.

BEELZEBUB
(He attacks Michael from behind. lucifer regains stability and wages a severe strike against Michael till he becomes weak to retaliate)

MICHAEL
(Michael calls for help from Elohim).

Arise! Arise! Jehovah Sabaoth.
Let your enemies be scattered
Lord of lords, Lord of hosts!
Let your enemies be overpowered.

ELOHIM
(Speaking from his throne).

Michael —
My brave and great warrior
Peace, your might is very superior.
Every villain has a flaw or weakness

Victory is assured, they will speechless.

LUCIFER
(To Elohim)

Your commander is useless
Promising them victory is needless.
Come and fight if you are a true king.
War is the pride of every leader or king.

ELOHIM
(Elohim resurrects all the slain army, forms one strong warrior by the name of Merkabah)

Adieu, Lucifer!
You have fallen from grace.
Before my judgment seat is your case
Adieu! You have fallen from grace!

(Enter Merkabah to fight alongside Michael and Gabriel).

MERKABAH
(To Michael)

Michael—
Take this sword, it's the Cross Of Light
Darkness can't withstand light.
Lucifer and his military shall faint.
They hate light, it will be their end!

(Suddenly, a special sword like the cross of light appears to Michael, Gabriel, and his military).

LUCIFER
(His military crying in defeat, all their weapons begin to melt like ice under sun)

(Beelzebub, Lucifer and other commanders Surrender)

ELOHIM

(To Michael).

> Enough! Enough! Enough!
> Halt the fight, take them captive
> Strip Lucifer of everything attractive.
> Escort him to the court-martial
> He will be judged with nothing partial.

(Exeunt, Michael, Gabriel, Merkabah, and defeated army before the judgement seat of Elohim).

[Court-Martial].
[A Judgment Room
In The Extraterrestrial World or Heaven]

*(Enter Elohim, Michael, Raphael, Uriel, Gabriel, Metatron,
Merkabah, and other loyal heavenly hosts)*

*(Chorus continues with the cherubim, singing, flapping
their six wings, flying around, and all the throne).*

CHORUS

Holy, Holy, Holy, our Sovereign Lord,
In reverent praise, our hearts are poured.
From the dawn of time to eternity's end,
Our worship to you, O King, shall transcend.

In every place, at each sacred hour,
Your name we exalt, our faith in you, our tower.
Eternal and timeless, your glory shines ever,
Our devotion to you will cease, never.

(Chorus Continues, Twenty-Four Elders Singing).

ELDERS

Worthy are You, Oh Great King
To receive honor, glory, and power...
You're, above all, all creatures before You sing.
You created all things and by your power
For Your praise, every creation's duty is to sing.

No creature ever determined Your will
For all You made, created were in Your perfect will.
You've written Your will in the Torah with a fire quill
You created us in love, in You alone is our being.

You're the Almighty, Your eyes all-seeing.

(Enter Elohim as consuming fire. From this fire is a gigantic book with the names of fallen angels with their judgment).

ELOHIM

I Am Who I Am
I Am King Elohim!
I am the Supreme Law of all laws
I am the supreme Judge of all judges.

Rebellion is an offense against my dignity
Worst of all, rebellion born from malicious conspiracy.
Lucifer, you have deceived many with malignity,
Before all creation, I pronounce you guilty.

Your place is no longer in my kingdom
I created you perfect with surpassing wisdom
But you wanted to be like the Most High
Your heart, you decided to corrupt and defile.

You were created of precious stones of fire
This made you proud with lustful desire
You denied prostrating before Adam
This, the highest disobedience to your doom.

I made him in my image for all to admire
But you argued he was made of clay and mire.
I will strip you of all honor and majesty
I will lower you less than clay in dignity.

(Chorus continues with the cherubim, singing, flapping their six wings, flying around, and all the throne).

CHORUS

Holy, Holy, Holy, our King most high,

To you, our praises shall ever fly.
You were, you are, and will be forever,
Our worship, unending, ceases never.

You, the King of justice, reign on high,
Supreme Judge, your wisdom fills the sky.
In all your judgments, truth does reflect,
Eternal worship, our gratitude we direct.

ELOHIM

I am who I am.
I am what I am.
I Am the Ancient of Days.
I Am the Father of All Lights.

I Am the El-Shaddai-The Almighty King.
I Am the Elohim-The Omnipotent King.
I Am the El-Elyon- The Most High King.
I Am El-Olam.The Everlasting King.

I Am the El-Roi-The King Who Sees.
I Am the King of Hosts.
I am Elohim Chayim - The Living God.
I am El Elyon - The Most High God.

ELDERS

(Repeating King Elohim's attributes with a louder male voice like an army ready for war).

You are the El-Shaddai
You are the Elohim
You are the El-Elyon
You are the El-Roi
You are the El-Olam.
You are the Lord of Hosts.

ELOHIM

I AM the sovereign King, Immutable,
I created the Earth and water indispensable,
I created the air and fire unquenchable,
I created day and created night irrefutable.

I created the seen and unseen undisputable,
I created light and darkness both mutable
I created the unseen in nine classes indisputable,
I created them in three orders so compatible.

I AM the sovereign King, Immutable,
I created them all perfect and so indispensable,
Cherubim, Seraphim, and Thrones, all suitable.
I created every creature after their kind suitable.

Cherubim, wisdom of my creation and motion,
Seraphim wisdom of creation, fiery motion.
Thrones, wisdom of creation, fixed motion,
My throne bearers, glorious, so imputable.

*(Chorus continues with the cherubim, singing, flapping
their six wings, flying around, and all the throne).*

CHORUS

You are El-Shaddai, provider and guide,
Elohim, our Creator, by your side.
El-Elyon, the Most High, you stand tall,
El-Roi, who sees us, hears our call.
El-Olam, eternal, your reign never ends,
Lord of Hosts, on you, our faith depends.

ELOHIM

(To Michael).

Bind Lucifer and his followers, let justice be served,
With searing fetters, their rebellion unnerved.
Cast them beyond Earth, to realms of endless dark,
Their defiance quelled, their fiery spark.

In the abyss, they shall find their abode,
Far from the heavens, in a desolate mode.
Their destiny sealed, an appointed time,
For their transgressions, they'll pay the crime.

(Lucifer, Beelzebub, and other are bound and cast out from heaven).

(Chorus Continues, Twenty-Four Elders Singing).

ELDERS

Worthy are You, O Great King on high,
To receive honor, glory, and power, we testify.
Above all, every creature does sing,
You formed all things, by Your mighty spring.

In praise, every creation's purpose takes wing,
For Your will, they harmoniously cling.
No creature can alter Your divine plan,
In Your love, our existence began.
You are the Almighty, all-seeing and supreme,
In You alone, we find our eternal dream.

(Enter Chorus by myriads of Angels)

Woe unto the Earth, woe unto the sea,
The devil has fallen with furious decree.
His wrath unleashed, a tempestuous tide,
In shadows he dwells, his malice cannot hide.

[EXEUNT]

ACT 4: SCENE 1

[Division of the Underworld Kingdom]

(Lucifer and his rebellious host are cast across seven divisions of hell, seven sub-divisions of hell, seven rivers of hell fire, seven rivers of hail fire).

REBEL

(Fighting amongst themselves…)

We were all deceived by Lucifer
To be cast into hell fire to suffer.
Our anguish is seven times tougher.
We will all perish altogether.

LUCIFER

Be calm, it is not time for remorse.
We have not even started our course.
The battle has just started
Be brave, don't be chicken hearted.

REBEL

Lucifer, we have lost the battle in heaven.
We have been cast into these hellish rivers.
We are in anguish; we are not good swimmers.
Let's plead for Elohim's mercy who delivers.

LUCIFER

I am your new king
I plan and decide on everything.
We will form a stronger kingdom
We will rule the world with wisdom.

REBEL

We are already defeated

Our fate has been decided.
We are doomed, what can we do?
We just wait for extinction when it's due.

LUCIFER

This day Elohim's name is forbidden,
I am your new King, the one unforbidden.
Forget all the past when were war-ridden,
Adam will soon suffer and be rag-ridden.

REBEL

Did you say Adam will be rag-ridden,
When myriads of angels secure Eden?
This seems a mission very impossible
Our plans too will be easily cognoscible.

LUCIFER

Our next operation must be top secret;
Everyone must be very discreet.
The fire of the fire awaits any traitor
Or anyone who becomes a perpetrator.

REBEL

We know he sees and knows all.
He can see anything big or even small.
How can we hide something in an open?
He can understand words even unspoken.

LUCIFER

He is King by himself, not for himself
Without his host, he can't pride himself.
He is bound by the Torah, his constitution
With free will, creation act by intuition.

REBEL

Adam is not an easy target to prey,

I am sure he knows he might be preyed.
Though he has a free will, he's intelligent
To detect anything that is belligerent.

LUCIFER

Don't forget that Eve is Adam's clown.
She was given to him as his crown.
But she will be the thorns to his flesh
Am I not worth more than king Gilgamesh?

REBEL

(Cheering)

LUCIFER

Remember Adam's first wife, Lilith
Whose heart I hardened like a trilith?
She rebelled against Adam for equality
And claimed her right with a rigid mentality…

REBEL

Lilith—
She must have taught Adam a lesson.
To reduce Adam's dignity and lessen.
Eve must have been told of Lilith's tale
To be watchful, not to falter and fail.

LUCIFER

Worry not, Eve is my toy.
I will break her into pieces like Troy.
I will take away her divine joy.
Though she pretends or is a coy.

REBEL

We think likewise.
Eve is vulnerable more or twice
She is easily beguiled and enticed.

Than Adam who is steadfast in paradise.

LUCIFER

My enemy king destroyed my light
But failed to destroy my insight.
My present sight can bring fright
To Eden's creature who see my sight.

REBEL

Insight is a tool useful, and your sight.
You can disguise as an angel of light
To enter Eden in other creature's body.
We can use any creature, a busybody.

LUCIFER

That's a good scheme to devise.
All we need now is to strategize.
My foe will soon be surprised
Adam's fall will make him more agonized.

REBEL

The serpent seems to be very crafty
Who can abase Eve in a way so nasty.
The serpent might know Eve's weakness
Which will cause her an eternal bleakness.

LUCIFER

I know the serpent is able
His desire for Eve is too insatiable.
Eve's conjugal life is something desirable
That the serpent has long seen as admirable.

REBEL

You have to befriend the serpent
Not as his master, but a servant.
He will take heed or be advertent

Eve's fall is inevitable, we're observant.

REBEL

(Yelling and shouting with joy)

Lucifer! Lucifer! Lucifer!
May you live forever!

[EXEUNT]

[Earth— Garden of Eden]

(Enter Elohim, Michael, Raphael, Uriel, Gabriel, and other loyal heavenly hosts to visit Adam in the garden of Eden).

(Chorus continues with the cherubim, singing, flapping their six wings, flying around, and all the throne).

CHORUS

Holy, Holy, Holy, our Sovereign King,
To you, our songs of praise we gladly bring.
You were, you are, and will forever be,
In worship, we find our hearts set free.

In every place, at every moment, we'll raise,
Our voices in worship, our songs of praise.
For your eternal reign, O King of grace,
We honor and adore in every sacred space.

(Suddenly a cloudy spiritual portal mirror with the colors of the rainbow or aura appears before Adam. Adam can see Elohim and the heavenly hosts all around Eden)

ADAM

Eve —
Haste, haste —
King Elohim is here
Elohim is here with the watchers…
Let's bow for him in holy fear

Open our hearts to his message hear,
He's the Alpha and the Omega
He has come for us to have fellowship
He has come with other companionship.

ELOHIM

Oh Adam! Father of many generations.
Your soul is the seed of many nations.
That which was from the foundations
I have to give you explanations.

ADAM

Oh Great King, the Almighty creator
You are the omniscience inventor
I shall heed to your word with attention
In your word, I shall delight without distraction.

ELOHIM

Your obedience is your redemption.
Your rebellion is your condemnation.
Your free will carries life and death
I have given you life through my breath.

ADAM

Oh, Great King!
Do not allow me to be tempted
Allow not my soul to be tainted.
For your name's sake, true and honorable,
Allow me not in any situation intolerable.

ELOHIM

No creation is exempted
What is good and virtuous is accepted.
What is evil is rewarded by punishment
The wages of sin in Eden is banishment.

ADAM

Oh great King! My limbs are terrified
My lips and tongue are petrified.
Why such prophecies of doom?

Has my soul offended you to merit the tomb?

ELOHIM

I am speaking for your posterity
I am speaking for their prosperity.
This is what will befall the soul of the pious
They have at their disposal abundance.

The pious shall traverse seven divine portals
Before they access the gate of the immortals.
The journey to Arabot or heaven will be merited,
Pious souls transformed to angels and exalted.

ADAM

Oh Great King!
Which are the portals?

ELOHIM

First portal—
The cave of Machpelah
The holy passage of Jehovah,
The welcoming portal of pious souls.

Second portal—
The gates of paradise
For the souls who will earn righteousness,
Guarded by the cherubim's flaming sword.
Third portal— Zebul
The gate of heaven.
In its abode I have constructed mansions
A reward settlement for the righteous.

If worthy, Michael guards the soul
The Earth is a little seed of my kingdom;
To the seventh portal —
The Shekinah glory.

The voice of the tree is calling
The fruit of the tree is cajoling
Woe unto you if you are enticed
Woe unto you if you think you'll be wise.
You will lose paradise, you'll lose paradise.

The voice of the tree is calling
The fruit of the tree is appealing
But woe unto if you eat
But woe unto if you eat it,
You will lose paradise, you'll lose paradise.

[EXEUNT
Back To Heaven]

[Earth— Outside The Garden Of Eden]

(Enter Lucifer as an angel of light, serpent is standing by the fence in Eden).

LUCIFER

The most honorable of all creation
I hail you above all veneration.
You are the crown of creation
You're a noble and worth admiration.

SERPENT

Such tributes are worth attention
From a prince of divine illumination.
What's the good news of your presence?
I am impatiently waiting with pleasance.

LUCIFER

Your destiny was stolen at creation
It was given to Adam for his adoration.
I am here to draw your attention
Of this hidden secret never mentioned.

SERPENT

You must be joking I assume?
A joke that can lead to one's doom…
What do you mean by stolen destiny?
Who might have stolen it, an enemy?

LUCIFER

More vicious than an enemy
Who created Adam to provoke envy.
And have you prostrate to this clay
Adam's creation is a script or by-play.

SERPENT

How do I know if this is accurate?
Before Adam, we always go prostrate.
He is our master; he gave me a name.
How can I blaspheme without shame?

LUCIFER

The violent take it by force
It is not time for you to remorse.
Look at your very essence or nature
Aren't you like Adam in feature?

SERPENT

Yes, you are right.
Something I thought of all nights.
Like Adam, I am gifted in intelligence
But I have wasted my honor by negligence.

LUCIFER

Eve is supposed to be your wife
You should not be living a lowlife.
Eve was created for your companionship
For a happy conjugal love relationship…

(Serpent feeling angry, jealous and remorseful).

SERPENT

What can I do to reclaim my right?
The right I owned by birthright?
I am glad you told me this mystery
I must seek ways for absolute recovery.

LUCIFER

We are in this battle together
I am your companion, don't be bitter

I will help you recover all for better.
I am all you need–you'll be better.

SERPENT

What is next, what do I need to do?
I must revenge for my breakthrough
Adam and Eve must pay the cost;
Even a lifetime is not too costly for this course.

LUCIFER

Lend me your body for this mission
We can combine our vision.
Two are better than one in any decision
We will strike Eve unfailingly with precision.

SERPENT

My body is yours any time
When you are ready, I don't mind
We can strike her anywhere in Eden.
I know where to find her in the Garden.

(*Lucifer enters the serpent*).

LUCIFER

Where is she now, any knowledge?
Do you know where she does lodge?
We need to target her when a lone
To deceive with knowledge unknown.

SERPENT

I know her too well and her forms
I will catch her - this be informed.
I know where she is fund of visiting
I know what she loves listening.

LUCIFER

I think I see someone like her
I see her standing so afar.
Could this be the time for us to act?
We must not waste time to attack.

SERPENT

Time is the not the best now
At such a time, Adam comes around.
We don't need to create any suspicion.
We must strike once with abscission.

LUCIFER

We shall wait in the morning
We shall strike hard without warning.
During the early hour of sun rise
Before the sun will fully arise…

SERPENT

I shall enter there like her good friend
Once Adam is gone the other end.
I will then entice her into transgression,
You sugar-coat after I get her attention.

LUCIFER
(Talking to himself within the serpent).

Eve, your end has come
I will play with your mind like a drum.
I will squash it in between my fingers,
You and Adam will be my beggars.

[EXEUNT]

ACT 4: SCENE 4

[Earth—Inside the Garden of Eden]

(V.O. by Metatron Continues)

(Enter chorus from myriads of Angels in Eden early in the morning).

    The voice of the tree is calling
    The fruit of the tree is cajoling
    Woe unto you if you are enticed
    Woe unto you if you think you'll be wise.
    You will lose paradise, you'll lose paradise.

    The voice of the tree is calling
    The fruit of the tree is appealing
    But woe unto if you eat
    But woe unto if you eat it,
    You will lose paradise, you'll lose paradise.

(Exeunt myriads of Angels, enter Lucifer in the body of the serpent).

SERPENT

Oh, my beloved mistress—
Mistress of the North and West
This day I have been so restless
But now I found you, I found rest.

EVE

Serpent, why are you restless?
Can you confide in me as your mistress?
Reveal to me the source of your distress.
I will be able to relieve your stress.

SERPENT

My Mistress, You're never seen all alone
Where have your guardian angels gone?
I feared for you when I saw you alone.
When I know you aren't too often alone.

EVE

Serpent, you are very observant,
You seem to know me well or conversant.
My guardian angels went to meet Elohim,
To make petitions on my behalf before him.

SERPENT

(Laughing)

My beloved mistress—
Did you say petition?

EVE

Yes, Serpent!
I said petition, what is funny?
Is there anything stupid or dummy?
What did I say that provokes laughter?
Stop! Express yourself to me better.

SERPENT

I want to tell you a story of a certain man.
He had superpowers such as superman.
He could create and destroy the worlds.
But he had a secret he hid from the worlds.

EVE

What secret was he hiding?
Was the secret so forbidding?
What on God's Earth will man be hiding?
Unless he was just a clown, just kidding.

SERPENT

He desired to be omnipotent
He exiled anyone claiming to be equipotent.
His secret was hidden on a tree…
Everyone could eat from it, it was free.

EVE

If the secret was hidden on a tree
If the tree itself was seen and for free,
Why did no one acquire the secret?
Was the power on the tree too sacred?

SERPENT

Mistress, very few people knew of this mystery.
You are now one of them with this mastery.
You can have these powers eating from it
It will grant you more powers and wit.

EVE

You must be a clown, kidding too!
Where is the tree if it is not new?
Let my eyes be my own witness
To confirm your story and its validness.

SERPENT
(Deliberately Pushing Eve Against A Tree)

My beloved mistress
Sorry for pushing you against the tree.
This is the tree I talked about, a mystery,
Very few know about it or its history.

EVE

Isn't this the tree in the middle of Eden?
Isn't this the forbidden tree of the Garden?

We can eat of every tree, but not this.
We shall die if we eat, we shall all decease.

SERPENT

No one dies by eating from a tree.
If you could die, why is the tree free?
Who told you all these invented lies?
The tree is here before all eyes.

EVE

King Elohim said we must not touch.
We could eat from other trees, but not of such.
The day we dare, we will surely die.
Death is not what I want now or desire.

SERPENT

My beloved mistress—
All lies! The fruit of this tree makes wise.
You become a demi-god otherwise.
You gain the power to create or destroy.
The world in your palms becomes a toy.

(Eve is hesitant).

You touched the tree but didn't die.
This already tells you it was a lie.
You can't die if you eat just a fruit.
Isn't a fruit considered as food?

EVE

But I am wise like my Lord Adam
Serpent, if it makes wise, why not Adam?
This Garden belongs to Elohim
You ought to show me by eating first.

SERPENT

I am not of mankind, with no power
I am not in the rulership but be ruled.
But you and Master Adam rule the world
Wisdom is set for your clan not ours.

(Enter Chorus)

The voice of the tree is calling
The fruit of the tree is cajoling
Woe unto you if you are enticed
Woe unto you if you think you'll be wise.
You will lose paradise, you'll lose paradise.

The voice of the tree is calling
The fruit of the tree is appealing
But woe unto if you eat
But woe unto if you eat it,
You will lose paradise, you'll lose paradise.

SERPENT
(Shaking off some fruits from the tree to fall on the ground).

My beloved mistress,
Here the fruit that carries grace,
One cannot be a coward for life -
You can have the power of afterlife.

Extra ordinary wisdom it will grace
Upon you and Adam over every creature.
Fear is your only foe to truly fear;
If you overcome fear, you will survive.

(He Picks up a very juicy fruit showing eve).

Elohim ate of this same tree and fruit
He's omnipotent, there is no chute.

Take this, eat with the heart of a god
Once you eat, you'll be a god with a rod.

(Giving one of the fruits to Eve).

My beloved mistress
Have a bite, or just a taste.
There is nothing to fear that you'll face.
Taste to be a goddess, do haste!

EVE
*(Eating the back of the fruit first, then gives it a bite,
 she gets naked, serpent smiles in admiration, Lucifer in
triumph).*

SERPENT
Adam must as well eat
Do not eat alone, let him have it.
You will have no other god to compete
You will all be fulfilled and complete.

(V.O. by Metatron Continues)

Eve was then beguiled by the serpent
The serpent disappeared unseen
She wept for the time spent
Serpent had vanished from the scene.

She wept bitterly for her greed
She wept bitterly for her seed.
She was now naked, very ashamed
She was now naked, who was to be blamed?

The trees shed their leaves in displeasure
The trees wept for Eve who lost her treasure.
Then Adam still working northward and ignorant,

For that only compassionate tree was the fig.

[EXEUNT]

[Earth—Inside the Garden of Eden]

(Eve Lures Adam to eat the fruit she just tested).

ADAM

Eve, why are you naked?
You were not this created?
Did you disobey Elohim's command?
Talk to me, I want to understand.

EVE

Adam, my husband, and my lord,
The master of and over creation;
I am doomed by the lust of my imagination.
The serpent beguiled with an holy revelation.

ADAM

What sacrilege have you committed?
It's sacrilegious and totally unaccepted.
Eating from that tree wasn't permitted.
How would you clear this and be acquitted.

EVE

The serpent persuaded me to eat,
The fruit was to make me wise and complete.
To be like a god with nobody to compete
Little did I know it was a lie, a mere deceit.

(Eve Weeping)

Elohim said we will surely die.
But this might truly have been a lie.
I ate the fruit, but I am still alive.

If I am alive, it means we can survive.

ADAM

Eve—
That could not have been a lie…
Why do you think of yourself this high?
We won't have been prohibited for nothing.
Of course, what else are you thinking?

EVE

If I did not die, it means it was a lie
You need to also eat, don't just deny.
I gave the fruit to other creation to also eat.
Most of them ate, they rejoiced, it was sweet.

ADAM

You have been corrupted Eve –
What is the base of such nerve?
You are naked before every creation –
You are the first such, in the whole garden.

EVE

It is true I am naked Adam,
All creatures appreciate the beauty
Don't you see what you don't see often?
Oh my Adam, just eat the fruit for me…

ADAM

Eve—
I don't want to die
Elohim said we will surely die.
Elohim is infallible to lie.
You rebelled, am not sure why.

EVE

(Weeping to entice Adam)

I see that you do not love me,
You have never truly loved me.
If I am still alive after eating this fruit
Why must you think as low as a brute?

ADAM

Eve my beloved—
It is not about love, but about obedience.
It is neither about death, nor expedience.
Elohim is our Master, King, and Creator
Why have you turned against him as a traitor?

EVE

(Angry, with seductive eyes)

All your speech is an exaggeration.
Your vision of death is a hallucination.
Everything is a mere fabrication
Eat the fruit, if you love me as a resolution.

(V.O. by Metatron Continues)

In honor of Eve's love and sobbing tears
And to please her, he drowned all his fears.
Adam also ate the forbidden fruit,
This was their final rebellion and chute.

They were all finally nude and naked.
Creation was shocked, and Elohim disappointed.
Then Michael sounded a trumpet to all the hosts.
All luminaries gathered from coast to coast.

The way the trumpet sounded this time
Was not normal, it foretold bad times to come.

They were to witness Adam's trial in Garden
After which they will be sent out of Eden.

*(Michael sounds a heavenly trumpet to summon all heavenly
hosts for the trial of Adam and eve in the garden).*

(Chorus by myriads of angels singing in lamentation).

Oh, Adam, Paradise is lost!
Oh Eve, Paradise is lost!
Why did you allow your lust
To cause a generation a great loss?

Your lust has caused your loss!
Your greed has caused your grief!
Why have you chosen perdition?
Why have you chosen damnation?

ADAM

(Adam is terrified and crying).

We're both naked, we're all naked!
We have violated what is sacred.
Woe unto us, woe unto us!
We've broken our covenant of divine trust.

EVE

We are only naked, but still alive
We will learn how to survive.
Let's haste, we can use fig leaves
For our covering and as our greaves.

(As they are rushing out).

ADAM

We have erred Eve, we have erred…

By ourselves, we have our fortunes ebbed.
I have broken the trust of Elohim…
We have shattered to confidence of Elohim.

[EXEUNT]

[Earth— Gates Garden of Eden]

(Enter chorus by the Cherubim, singing, flapping their six wings, and flying round and all around the throne).

CHORUS

Holy, Holy, Holy, our King divine,
To you, our praises and songs entwine.
You were, you are, and ever shall be,
In worship, we find our souls set free.

In every place, at each sacred hour,
With hearts ablaze, we feel your power.
Eternal and unchanging, your glory shines,
Our devotion to you, in endless lines.

ELOHIM

(Calling Adam from the East Gate of Eden).

Adam! Adam! Adam!
Where art thou?
Did you eat what was disallowed?
Adam! Adam! Where art thou?

ADAM

(Speaking from afar, ashamed and trembling and with a broken crying voice).

My King— My father,
I am here in the Garden's embrace,
I am here in Eden's sacred space,
But I am here in hiding, in shame's trace.

ELOHIM

Adam! Adam!
Where art thou?

ADAM

My King, my maker,
In the garden's quiet, I quiver.
I am ashamed and hiding,
From your gaze, my soul does shiver.

In Eden's realm, I once did roam,
In innocence, I called it home.
But now, in sin's embrace, I'm bound,
In shadows deep, I can't be found.

ELOHIM

Why are you in hiding?
Is there anything you're hiding so forbidding?
You used to welcome me with adoration
You used to welcome me with devotion?

ADAM

My king—
The woman you gave me as help
She has turned my joy into a bitter herb!
She enticed me and behold, I trespassed.
Here I am, in anguish and in an impasse.

ELOHIM

Adam—
Don't indict me for your transgression
I gave you my word to keep with discretion.
I gave you my word, not to Eve.
Didn't I give you wit to apperceive?

ADAM

(Adam is silent).

EVE

(In self-defense)

The serpent lured me to fall.
I was enticed, I was pushed to the wall.
He said the fruit will make me wise
Little did I know it was just vice.

ELOHIM

Adam—
I gave you Lilith,
She rebelled in insubordination
You prayed and wept in supplication.

I gave you Eve a woman of your admiration,
She was subordinate until your damnation.
What else can I bequeath to you Adam?
The heart of my garden you wounded Adam.

You gave it a bite, that wicked bite;
Because of unmoving tears, a bite…
Top my flesh and heart Eve had a bite,
Not yet absorbed the pain yours Adam, painful.

(Chorus by myriads of Angels, singing in the garden of Eden).

Oh, Adam, Paradise is lost!
Oh, Eve, Paradise is lost!
Why did you allow your lust
To cause a generation a great loss?

Your lust has caused your loss!
Your greed has caused your grief!
Why have you chosen perdition?
Why have you chosen damnation?

(At the center of Eden, under the tree where eve was deceived).

MICHAEL

(A book opens by Michael, the book of justice, judgement, and justice).

(V.O Metatron)

> *A book opens by Michael's hand so just,*
> *The tome of justice, judgment, and trust.*
> *Its pages whisper tales of right and wrong,*
> *As truth and fairness in its verses throng.*
>
> *Inscribed within, the stories of our deeds,*
> *The scales of justice, where virtue leads.*
> *With wisdom's quill, its chapters are penned,*
> *The Book of Justice, where all souls contend.*

(Chorus Continues, Twenty-Four Elders Singing).

ELDERS

> Worthy are You, Oh Great King on high,
> To receive honor, glory, and power, we comply.
> Above all, every creature in chorus rings,
> You formed all things, as the universe sings.
>
> For Your praise, every creation's voice does spring,
> In harmonious praise, their anthem they bring.
> No creature could ever shape Your divine plan,
> In Your love, our existence began.
>
> In the Torah's sacred script, Your will unfolds,
> With a fire quill, its truth it upholds.
> In Your love, we find our very being,
> You're the Almighty, with all-seeing eyes, foreseeing.

(Enter Sanhedrin of seventy-one angels during the judgment of Adam, Eve, Serpent. A book is book like a scroll from which the judgement of is read and pronounced).

ELOHIM

None has shown me any penitence
My mercy surpasses my judgment
I sought a contrite heart or repentance
To avert my wrath and pre-judgment.

I found none in Adam except a heart conceited.
I found none in Eve except a heart arrogated.
Today, my judgment is officially announced
Today, my judgment is officially pronounced.

(Chorus continues with the cherubim, singing, flapping their six wings, flying around, and all the throne).

CHORUS

Holy, Holy, Holy, our King so divine,
To you, our praises forever entwine.
You were, you are, and shall ever be,
In worship, our souls find eternity's key.

In every place, at each sacred hour,
With reverence, we feel your power.
Eternal and unchanging, your glory does shine,
Our devotion to you, an eternal lifeline.

(Sanhedrin of seventy-one angels, waiting to execute Elohim's judgment once pronounced)

ELOHIM

(To Adam, angrily).

Adam here is your sentence
You've lost your divine raiment.
You shall eat bread with no merriment
Your daily food will now be perishable.

Your seed will be wanderers in strange lands
They will be enslaved from your sin inheritable.
Your body will ooze smell from sweat glands,
Your heart will be given to evil proclivities.

Today I take away preservation and ease,
Maggots will feast on your dead body and carcass.
Animals will be your master with hostilities,
Paradise will be lost, and you will be banished.

ELOHIM

(To Eve)

Eve, here is your sentence, spoken clear,
In childbirth, you shall toil and fear.
Your offspring's birth will bring you pain,
As I replace joy with labor's strain.

Through travail, you'll tread close to death's door,
Seeking my aid for health and more.
Your desire shall turn to your husband's care,
Affection growing like wildfire, a love to bear.

ELOHIM

(To the serpent).

Serpent, you who bore the evil seed,
For your jealousy, here is your sentence;
I made you head of all beasts …
Iniquity in your heart grew like yeast.

After Adam, you were the best in creation,
I gave you features worth every admiration.
I created you upright, to walk like a man
I created you to eat the same food with man.

Your heart became conceited and hardened.
Today, your sentence is with no pardon
You lusted and coveted Eve, Adam's wife.
Her seed will be to you like a sharp knife.

You shall be a woman and her seed's enemy
The woman's seed will also be your archenemy
You shall crawl on your belly, no more legs
You shall now eat dust, no more eggs.

(Silence for a while)

ELOHIM

(To Adam)

Though you have lost paradise and Eden
By accepting to eat the fruit evil and forbidden,
I will not forsake you for your contrite heart.
I will build you a cave, mighty and hard.

The cave will be your temporal shelter
Till your redeemer comes as your helper.
Though the Earth be filled with terror
And pestilence due to your error

None shall come near your dwelling cave.
None shall send you to an early grave.
I will love you as your eternal King and Father.
I will preserve as father under my feather.

(Adam bows down before King Elohim in reverence)

Oh, Great King and Mighty Elohim so grand,
What is man, that you hold him in your hand?
You've made him lower than the angels above,
Yet in majesty and grace, you fill him with love.

Cloaked in splendor, beyond what angels bear,
Man's spirit shines with a radiance rare.
Though humble in form, he possesses divine might,
In your image, he walks, in your glorious light.

ELOHIM

(To Michael, Lucifer, and Gabriel)

Build him a cave of treasures.
Where he fill find rest and pleasure.
Build him a cave, east of the Garden
Where paradise was lost with Eden.

Let the cave always be sanctified
By your prayers, it will be purified.
There in shall dawn a new generation
Until the day of you full redemption.

Once paradise lost is regained
You shall return to the Garden of Eden again.
This is for a time unknown and undefined.
When prophecy be fulfilled and re-aligned.

(Chorus Continues, Twenty-Four elders singing).

Worthy, worthy, worthy, we proclaim,
The Lamb who was slain, in His name.
His kingdom shall forevermore reign,

In His honor, we lift our joyful strain.

Worthy is the Lamb, His power to attain,
With honor and wisdom, His glory shall sustain.
An everlasting kingdom, His righteous domain,
In the blood of life, His love does remain.

(V.O. by Metatron Continues)

So Adam and Eve
Were exiled from the Garden of Eden
Their hearts were broken and smitten.
The serpent lost his beauty and legs

He also lost eating good food like eggs,
Now bound in reproduction to lay eggs.
He was to crawl on the ground with his belly
His damnation and fall was mocked by all.

(Chorus Continues, Twenty-Four Elders Singing)

ELDERS

Worthy are You, Oh Great King, sublime,
To receive honor, glory, throughout all time.
Above all, creatures harmonize and sing,
In Your creation's symphony, praises ring.

No creature's will can change Your divine plan,
All formed by Your perfect will, since time began.
In the Torah's sacred words, Your will is instilled,
In love, we're fashioned, with purpose fulfilled.

You're the Almighty, with omniscient sight,
In Your presence, we find eternal light.
In worship and awe, our voices raise,

For Your majesty and love, we offer praise.
[EXEUNT]

[An Extraterrestrial Kingdom]

(At The Gates Of Heaven).

MICHAEL

(Stops Lucifer at the gate).

Heaven is no longer your dwelling
Why are you here arrogant and yelling?
Have you not caused enough damage?
For you to still be going on rampage?

LUCIFER

I am glad I caused a lot of damage.
I am neither here for any homage.
I am sure Elohim is still in rage.
We can still write a new page.

MICHAEL

You have long been defeated.
History cannot be repeated.
Light has nothing to do with darkness
Light is all about righteousness.

LUCIFER

Elohim—
Is the reason why I am here
Tell him I am here, let him not fear.
My proposal for him is simple and clear.
A tête a tête with not want to interfere.

(Enter Elohim, seraphim pulling his throne)
(Gate of heaven, exit Michael).

CHORUS

Holy, Holy, Holy, our King on high,
With praises and songs, to you, we draw nigh.
You were, you are, and will forever be,
In worship, our souls find eternity.

In every place, at every sacred hour,
With reverence, we feel your mighty power.
Eternal and unchanging, your glory does gleam,
Our devotion to you, a perpetual stream.

MICHAEL

You are too feeble to make Elohim fear –
A servant only you have been to bring fear.
He is all-knowing and all-powerful
Lucifer, you are under mercy to be in hell.

LUCIFER

Well—
I am here for a friendly visit,
Though inhibited at the gate as my limit.
In brief, I noticed you had a feast
I wasn't invited, perhaps — I am a beast!

ELOHIM

I created you not as a beast.
You shone like the sun from the east.
You corrupted other creation
For them to share in your damnation.

LUCIFER

Good memory lane of history,
What matters was the victory.
Besides, Adam is now my slave.
He will rot in the grave.

ELOHIM

Why are you here in such ugly state?
With a free will, you chose your fate.
Repentance or amends are too late.
You will just have to accept your fate.

LUCIFER

I am here to accuse the clay you set to challenge me
I entered the snake every did trust and admire
And brought damnation upon them…
Though I know your heart still beats for Adam.

ELOHIM

I hold his destiny and posterity,
He blundered only a moment, not for eternity.
The lamb had been slain from the foundation
He might have sinned, but not unto damnation.

LUCIFER

Keep your lamb!
Adam is my sacrificial lamb.
Here is my proposal for an exchange,
I hope you won't find it strange?

ELOHIM

Everything about you is strange
Pride had long made you derange.
Can good come out of darkness?
Do you need healing for your madness?

LUCIFER

Why not restore my beauty?
Why not restore my dignity?
Adam will be released freely
He's my lawful captive so ideally.

ELOHIM

You have no legal right to demands here
For you were never material for an heir.
You have corrupted the heavens and the Earth
But you will not be qualified even for the Earth.

LUCIFER

What is the use of Adam to you
A mere mortal who can't keep instructions?
An object easily beguiled by seductions?
You should have thought this in his formation.

ELOHIM

You betrayed me, conspired against me…
You betrayed the celestial realm
And brought disorder right to my face,
But Adam only disobeyed me, you see….

LUCIFER

But now, I have him under captivity,
Restore me and I will release him…
For even your peace will be in captivity,
I will cause the heart you have for Adam bleed.

ELOHIM

You are designed for hell and doom
In my kingdom, you have no room.
Adam might be enslaved, but one who is free
He whom the son of man sets free
Is indeed and forever free—

LUCIFER

If I am doomed for hell,
So is Adam who likewise fell.
Who then is the first to visit hell?
I, or Adam whom you love so well?

ELOHIM

Adam might be a lawful captive,
But his captivity is redemptive.
I catch the wise in their craftiness.
I destroy and expose all their shadiness.

(Chorus Continues, Twenty-Four elders singing).

Worthy, worthy, worthy, we proclaim,
The Lamb who was slain, in His name.
His kingdom shall forevermore reign,
In His honor, we lift our joyful strain.

Worthy is the Lamb, His power to attain,
With honor and wisdom, His glory shall sustain.
An everlasting kingdom, His righteous domain,
To Him be praise, in His eternal reign.

ELOHIM

It will interest you to know that Adam
Only disobeyed, lured by your sham,
But never rebelled against his creator,
He never raised men to rival his creator.

LUCIFER

If Adam could fail his mission,
The lamb will fail without any option.
Don't put all your heart and trust
In your lamb, I will cause him to rust.

ELOHIM

A liar you are, and father of all lies.
But truth in the bosom of the lamb lies.
Your doom or destruction is inevitable.
Before his own foes, I will dress him a table.

LUCIFER

You have turned down my request,
This was my final wish and quest.
My sword for revenge is eager and ready.
To kill, steal and destroy anyone greedy.

ELOHIM

I give you many years to struggle in your evil
But only the rotten like Beelzebub joins a devil.
Adam is made in my image, my light on him…
My hand is upon Adam and his generations.

(Exit Lucifer, very furious).

(Chorus Continues, Twenty-Four elders singing).

Worthy, worthy, worthy, we sing in praise,
The Lamb who was slain, our voices raise.
His kingdom shall reign for eternity's span,
Worthy is the Lamb, our Sovereign and plan.

To Him be power, honor, and wisdom profound,
In His everlasting kingdom, truth shall resound.
The Lamb who was slain, our Savior and guide,
In His glory and grace, forever shall abide.

[EXEUNT ELOHIM
and Heavenly Hosts]

[Earth —
Cave of Adam and Eve's Dwelling]

(Adam and eve are now exposed to real life out of the garden, where they now fend for themselves. Eve is full of regret and bitterness for her error).

EVE
(Eve Weeping)
My lord Adam, my soul is so much in anguish.
My strength is sapped, I am famished.
All my fault that we have been banished
Oh my soul, oh my soul, I'm languished.

ADAM
The fault isn't just yours, but mine.
Don't let anguish eat up your mind.
We are all guilty, we all did fail.
King Elohim remains our bail.

EVE
My lord Adam, how I long for our redemption…
For seven days we are in starvation?
How long, how long shall we have our salvation?
O my soul, why did I bring this damnation?

ADAM
My love, we are of clay, we are all frail
No need to weep, no need to wail.
Elohim is merciful in compassion
Let's hold steadfast to our confession.

EVE

Let me offer myself to you as a sacrifice
Slay me to death, if this will suffice,
To avert and appease this suffering.
My Lord, use me for your drink offering.

ADAM

My love—
We must not despair, though starving,
We all erred by greed and craving.
Let me go hunt for food in the field.
Be brave, be brave, don't yield.

(Flashback)

My Eve, think of the night of our oath…
The night in which we did betroth,
You promise me your eternal love.
For love, I ate the fruit forbidden from above.

EVE

I am guilty of such woeful reminiscent
I blamed the serpent, an act indecent.
To take the guilt off your shoulder
But my Lord, justice prevailed even harder.

ADAM

My love, you were right, you did not lie,
You were enticed by the serpent's lie.
Elohim's enemy, Lucifer, is very sly,
Beware, he roams always as a spy.

(Exit Adam to look for food, enter Lucifer).

LUCIFER

Dear Eve,
Do you know you are a traitor?
You betrayed the love of your creator?
You caused Adam's penury
You are responsible for his injury.

EVE

What do you want from me?
Why have you decided to be mean?
You caused my downfall from Eden.
You lured me to what was forbidden.

LUCIFER

Dear Eve, forget this past predicament
Let's talk about this moment.
Do you think Adam will still love you?
His love for you is no longer true?

EVE

(Eve begins to sob).

LUCIFER

The truth is always bitter,
Two bitter truths aren't better.
Elohim can never forgive you.
Neither Adam will ever forgive you.

EVE

I wish death had swallowed me
I wish I were swallowed by the sea?
I wish the sun could burn to ash.
My punishment is too hard and harsh.

LUCIFER

Wise Eve, death is never too late.
Everyone around you is full of hate.

Elohim hates you, just your mate.
Why not commit suicide as your fate?

*(The voice of Adam calling from outside the cave, exit Lucifer,
enter Adam).*

ADAM

Still— sobbing?
Cheer up, let's keep hoping.
We have already been chastised.
Keep hope and faith to be energized.

EVE

My strength is not eternal.
My strength is only ephemeral.
Did you find any food in the field?
I am dead alive; this is how I feel.

ADAM

The field wasn't gracious
I could not find any food precious.
Like any food we had in the Eden.
I am hungrified; I am hunger smitten!

EVE

All my fault! All my fault!!!
That by greed I did exalt pride
All my fault! All my fault!!!
I did fail you as your bride.

ADAM

Elohim is merciful and gracious
His law and promises are precious.
Let us beat our breast.
For his mercy's sake and rest.

The Almighty King our maker…
The merciful King, our creator
Remember us, O infallible King
That we are clay, we are mortal vessels.

We have already been broken at all levels.
Your chastisement is true and holy.
Your justice is true and wholly.
We are vessels of flesh and unholy.

You alone are righteous, we're filthy,
Who else can we run to, your mercy.
Turn your face on our destitution,
Deliver us from hunger execution.

You created and honored us
Despite our weakness you set us platform,
Even Angels bowed at the mention of us –
I take responsibility for our disobedience.

We only ask for your mercy
Chastise us but show us mercy.
Bypass even our clay nature as before
And show us mercy in your goodness.

(Suddenly trees field begin to grow food, enter Michael, and other heavenly hosts)

(Chorus Continues myriads of Angels).

Worthy, worthy, worthy, we declare,
The Lamb who was slain, His name we share.
His kingdom, eternal, shall evermore stand,

Worthy is the Lamb, at His throne we'll band.

To Him belong power, honor, wisdom divine,
In His everlasting kingdom, His light will shine.
The Lamb who was slain, our Savior and Lord,
In His presence, our praises are joyfully poured.

MICHAEL

Your penance has ascended like incense.
Elohim has forgiven your offense.
You must remain pious in his presence.
His WORD, TORAH is your only defense.

*(Adam and Eve become excited and the radiance is seen on
their faces).*

[EXEUNT]

ACT 5: SCENE 4

[An Extraterrestrial Kingdom]

(Enter myriads of mourning Angels).

HOSTS

O Adam! O Adam!
How art thou fallen?
How art thou fallen?

Our master Adam is fallen
The voice of a creation is calling
The voice of creation is weeping
The voice of creation is wailing.

We're sorrowful, but hopeful
We're sorrowful, but hopeful

(Enter King Elohim, followed by Cherubim pulling the throne).

MICHAEL

My King, the soul of Adam is in anguish.
He has become feeble and languish.
Great King, show him mercy and kindness
So his soul might find joy and happiness.

ELOHIM

Weep not for worthy is the lamb
That will in due season be his lamp.
The lamb was slain before the foundation.
Only the lamb can atone for his redemption.

Worthy, worthy, worthy, we acclaim,
The Lamb who was slain, in His name.
The light of the world, our guiding lamp,
In His glory, we find our camp.

Worthy, worthy, worthy, indeed,
The Lamb who can open the scroll, take heed.
Omnipotent, with power to control,
In His majesty, He makes us whole.

Worthy, worthy, worthy, it's known,
The Lamb who opens all seals, His throne.
He crushes the serpent, his power wanes,
In victory, our Savior forever reigns.

Worthy! Worthy! Worthy!
Is the lamb who can open all seals
And crush the serpent under his heels

ELOHIM

Without blood, there is no sin atonement.
Without blood, there is no re-enthronement.
Without blood, my wrath can't be appeased,
Without blood, Adam can't be at ease.

Without blood, sins are not forgiven
Without the blood hope is void for the living.
Without blood, there is no healing
Without blood, there no righteousness
Without blood, there is no forgiveness.

(Chorus Continues, Twenty-Four elders singing).

Worthy! Worthy! Worthy!

Is the lamb that was slain
Whose kingdom for ever will reign.
Worthy is the lamb that was slain,
To receive power, honor, and wisdom
Whose reign is an everlasting kingdom.
Life is in the blood of every living thing…

ELOHIM

On that will be a new heaven!
On that will be a new haven!
My tabernacle will be with man
I will be the King for my remnant.

I will wipe their tears and be their consolation
I will wipe their tears, no more desolation.
Death will be swallowed in victory
Their seed will remember me in all history.

(Chorus Continues, Twenty-Four Elders Singing)

ELDERS

Worthy are You, Oh Great King on high,
To receive honor, glory, that never will die.
Above all, creation in reverence shall sing,
For You created all things, under Your wing.

No creature's will changed Your divine decree,
In Your perfect will, all came to be.
In the Torah's sacred words, Your wisdom instilled,
In love, You shaped us, with purpose fulfilled.

You're the Almighty, with omniscient sight,
In Your presence, we find eternal light,
The Almighty, the eyes all-seeing,
To You, our praises, we're forever bringing.

ELOHIM

I am who I am.
I am what I am.
I Am the Ancient of Days.
I Am the Father of All Lights.

I Am the El-Shaddai-The Almighty King.
I Am the Elohim-The Omnipotent King.
I Am the El-Elyon- The Most High King.
I Am El-Olam.The Everlasting King.

I Am the El-Roi-The King Who Sees.
I Am the King of Hosts.
I am Elohim Chayim - The Living God.
I am El Elyon - The Most High God.

(Chorus continues with the cherubim, singing, flapping their six wings, flying around, and all the throne).

CHORUS

Holy, Holy, Holy, our King so great,
To you, we offer our praises and await,
You were, You are, and forever will be,
In worship, our souls find eternity.

In every place, at every sacred hour,
With hearts ablaze, we feel your power,
Eternal and unchanging, your glory does gleam,
Our devotion to you, an eternal stream.

ADAM

(Adam, imploring Elohim's mercy while the gathering takes place in heaven).

Almighty King—
May you live forever and ever

For your word and dominion lasts forever
You are the wisest of all, the most clever.

Your judgment and justice is right
Your mercy and justice is what I delight.
Remember, oh Great King, we are clay
One day, Eve and I will get rotten or decay.

How can clay be righteous before his potter?
Show us mercy, that we might live forever.
We were deceived by the serpent, and we fell
We lost Paradise - Eden, in which we used to dwell.

Only you can determine the end from beginning,
Mighty King, I lay down all before you for mercy,
Do not forsake us, O merciful great King
Our soul is anguished, no song of joy to sing.

ELOHIM

(Sending Michael to Adam)

Michael, I have heard Adam's supplication.
Haste to him with my consolation.
Cloth him with animals skin
That peace will suffice his chagrin.

Bring them up for the heavenly Sabbath.
The Sabbath was made for man,
Not man for the Sabbath,
My image is in him, he is mine.

(Exit Michael, re-enter along with the soul and spirit Adam and Eve. First Sabbath after creation. Heavenly Celebration With Singing).

(Chorus continues with the cherubim, singing, flapping their six wings, flying around, and all the throne).

CHORUS

Holy, Holy, Holy, Is Our King,
Unto you shall we praise and sing.
Who was, and is, and lives forever.
We shall worship you wherever and whenever.

ELOHIM

(To Adam)

A contrite heart is what I desire
Burnt offering is none of my desire.
Repentance will bring you higher
Repentance will always renew your fire.

ADAM

Blessed is he whom you chastise.
Your justice I will never despise.
Blessed is he whose fault or transgression
Are forgiven, covered in true confession.

ELOHIM

(Flashback: To Adam)

Though you have lost paradise and Eden
By accepting to eat the fruit evil and forbidden,
I will not forsake you for your contrite heart.
I will build you a cave, mighty and hard.

The cave will be your temporal shelter
Till your redeemer comes as your helper.
Though the Earth be filled with terror
And pestilence due to your error

None shall come near your dwelling cave.
None shall send you to an early grave.
I will love you as your eternal King and Father.
I will preserve as father under my feather.

(Adam bow down before King Elohim in reverence)

(Enter Chorus Myriads of Angels)

Oh Great King and Mighty Elohim so high,
Why do you remember man with a watchful eye?
You made him lower than angels, we understand,
But clothed in majesty beyond what we'd planned.

Though humble in form, he's bestowed with grace,
A creation of wonder, in this earthly place.
In Your image, he stands, a reflection so bright,
With potential and purpose, in Your divine light.

ELOHIM
(To Michael, Lucifer, and Gabriel)

Build him a cave of treasures.
Where he fill find rest and pleasure.
Build him a cave, east of the Garden
Where paradise was lost with Eden.

Let the cave always be sanctified
By your prayers, it will be purified.
There in shall dawn a new generation
Until the day of you full redemption.

Once paradise lost is regained
You shall return to the Garden of Eden again.
This is for a time unknown and undefined.
When prophecy be fulfilled and re-aligned.

(Chorus Continues, Twenty-Four elders singing).

Worthy! Worthy! Worthy!
Is the lamb that was slain
Whose kingdom for ever will reign.

Worthy is the lamb that was slain,
To receive power, honor, and wisdom
Whose reign is an everlasting kingdom.
Life is in the blood of every living thing…

[EXEUNT]

EPILOGUE

(V.O. by Metatron Continues)

A tragic story of a King and father,
Whose kingdom was fought by a watcher.
There were many watchers like lucifer
But lucifer's pride made him see too far.

Elohim created the world with his wisdom
Adam was created to rule over his kingdom.
Lucifer was both an archangel and a seraphim
Similar to Michael, all were created by Elohim.

He was elegant; he was also the Light Bearer
But his light was to bring more terror.
He was created perfectly, with no error
He was the wisest of all watchers, a torch bearer.

He had no equal, except Elohim, his superior,
He was the bright light to shine the star
Who could change to any desired avatar
The most stately their kind, and the brightest star.

His wings were colossal and looked like gold,
His eyes could sometimes glow like burning coal.
He had younger siblings created after him
Gabriel, Raphael, Uriel, all by King Elohim.

He tried to entice them into his insurrection.
Michael and Gabriel resisted as his opposition.
Lucifer argued that God was a tyrant or dictator
Who wanted to assume all powers as a sole creator.

He became the voice of rebellion in heaven.
And planted discord in many hearts as a leaven.
He hated the creation of Adam and humanity
And opposed this creation with profanity.

Adam was made of Elohim's image and clay
An inferior substance that will soon decay.
He was created perfect, and more so with fire.
How could fire prostrate to clay or even admire?

Lucifer bore contempt for both Elohim and Adam
Then started plotting Adam's Adam fall.
He had gained support to wage a war,
But I wonder who wins his creator in a war.

He had turned the heart of many watchers
Who now became Elohim's ill-wishers.
With a growing army, war was now inevitable,
He had enticed a great number, so unbelievable.

These were willing to fight for independence,
His army was huge to break any resistance.
Lucifer was the main commander in chief
Beelzebub the second commander in chief.

Samuel led an army to destroy Elohim's throne,
He raged against any Empyrean guard known.
He fought to pave the way for Lucifer
Inflicting Empyrean guards with pain to suffer.

While Michael, Uriel, and other angels fought
Elohim was the main target in Lucifer's thought.
He entered the Empyrean for a face to face
Combat with Elohim, wishing to have him erased.

Gabriel appeared, requested a war cessation,
But Lucifer was not ready for any war termination.
Lucifer enraged, marched toward Elohim's throne
Cleared every resistance, from both known and unknown
Gabriel resisted Lucifer's great army and might;
Beelzebub joined lucifer to push forth the fight.

Gabriel was defeated, and Lucifer met Elohim.
Elohim was on his throne, surrounded by seraphim.
He was peaceful, then asked Lucifer to repent.
Lucifer reposted with a heart full of contempt.

Beelzebub and Lucifer were ready to strike
The throne of Elohim for which they had dislike.
Michael then appeared and overpowered them,
Destroyed Lucifer's battalions many of them.

The battle was fierce, defaulters to be condemned,
Defeated by Elohim's throne before being condemned,
Michael pleaded with Lucifer to repent,
Lucifer again in pride did not sow consent.

Lucifer appealed to Samuel
Who came in as the Great Dragon
To wage war against the archangel Michael;
But the host was fortified with Angel Raphael.

The dragon was so powerful to overcome
A fierce war with an unpredictable outcome.
Michael was soon exhausted and weak
A chance for Lucifer and Samuel to strike quick.

Suddenly, Archangel Merkabah joined Michael
A formidable force to subdue Lucifer and Samuel.
Michael regained his strength with a Cross of Light

He then faced Lucifer and Samuel with great might.

Elohim the Great and the Captain of the Host
Seated on the throne and watching;
Seeing the Cross of Light, Lucifer was exhausted.
Samuel, the great dragon, was also defeated.

Lucifer and his angels were cast from heaven.
They had no place to go, no abode, or haven.
The war wasn't yet over, there was another war.
The conquest of the abyss, the forging hell.

These were creations Elohim made with love
Who rose up with evil to contest against love.
The porter can always make another
When the branch of a tree feels bigger.

END OF VOLUME ONE

WATCHOUT

FOR VOLUME TWO!!!

JUDE 1:6

"…And the angels which kept not their first estate, but left their own habitation, he hath reserved in everlasting chains under darkness unto the judgment of the great day…"

King James Bible

OTHER BOOKS

1. Miss Angel: *The Evil Behind the Law Vol. I.* (Verse Drama)
2. Ms. Angel: *The Evil Behind the Law Vol. II.* (Verse Drama)
3. Miss Seraphim *The Evil Behind the Law Vol. III.* (Verse Drama)
4. The Cosmos and Spiritual Warfare. (Christian Lit in Prose)
5. The Lost Kingdom Lineage. (Christian Lit in Prose)
6. The Poesy of Diaspora Poetry (Collection of Poetry)
7. Paradise Lost & the Watchers of Heaven I. (Christian Sci-Fi)
8. Paradise Lost & the Watchers of Heaven II. (Christian Sci-Fi)
9. Paradise Lost & the Watchers of Heaven III. (Animated Sci-Fi)
10. Paradise Lost & the Watchers of Heaven IV. (Animated Sci-Fi)
11. Ms. Angel's Poet: Verse Autobiography
12. Embracing Creative Transformation